GAMER SQUAD 1

Attack of the Not-So-Virtual Monsters

KIM HARRINGTON

STERLING CHILDR
New Yo

STERLING CHILDREN'S BOOKS
New York

An Imprint of Sterling Publishing Co., Inc.
1166 Avenue of the Americas
New York, NY 10036

STERLING CHILDREN'S BOOKS and the distinctive
Sterling Children's Books logo are registered trademarks of
Sterling Publishing Co., Inc.

ISBN 978-1-4549-2612-2

Distributed in Canada by Sterling Publishing Co., Inc.
c/o Canadian Manda Group, 664 Annette Street
Toronto, Ontario, Canada M6S 2C8
Distributed in the United Kingdom by GMC Distribution Services
Castle Place, 166 High Street, Lewes, East Sussex, England BN7 1XU
Distributed in Australia by NewSouth Books
45 Beach Street, Coogee, NSW 2034, Australia

For information about custom editions, special sales, and premium
and corporate purchases, please contact Sterling Special Sales at
800-805-5489 or specialsales@sterlingpublishing.com.

Manufactured in Canada

Lot #:
2 4 6 8 10 9 7 5 3 1
06/17

sterlingpublishing.com

Design by Ryan Thomann

To Mike and Ryan,
my favorite gamers

1

The monster had a penguin's body, a unicorn's head, and sharp fangs. It bounced from one webbed foot to the other. The little beast was taunting me, right there on the sidewalk in front of my own house. But I'd get it.

I narrowed my eyes and concentrated. The late afternoon sun burned against my back, and a bead of sweat dripped down from my forehead into my eyes. But I didn't blink. I acted.

With a quick swipe of my finger, I launched a BattleNet. The monster ducked. I swiped again, anticipating its next move, and *BAM!* Caught!

My best friend, Charlie, whooped and hollered from over my shoulder. "Yeah, Bex! You got it!"

I gave Charlie a little smile, but I didn't feel a huge sense of satisfaction. I'd caught Uniguins before. They were common in our neighborhood. I wanted to catch something better, like a VampWolf. I'd only caught one of those.

I reached up and tightened my ponytail. On humid days like today, my mess of long, brown curls seemed to double in size. "Want to walk to the park and see if there are better monsters there?"

Charlie held up the cellphone in his hand and waved it back and forth. "My hour is up. I have to return this to my mom."

Oh, right. *Monsters Unleashed* was a mobile game, and while I was lucky—twelve years old with my own phone—Charlie had to borrow his mom's. So he could only play for short periods.

"I guess I'll go home and bring it back," he said, looking up at his house but not moving his feet. His older brother's bike was in the driveway. And when

Jason Tepper Jr. was home, that meant Charlie would be tortured.

"Do you want to come over after?" I asked. "I think my mom made lemonade and cookies today."

Charlie's face lit up. "That sounds great! See you in a minute."

He ran to his house, his sneakers kicking up dirt, and I started walking to mine. Charlie and I had been friends since I moved into the house next door to his when I was five. He was always around and more than willing to play or hang out.

We'd finished elementary school about a month ago and would be entering seventh grade at the end of the summer. Middle school. Sometimes I worried that things wouldn't be the same in our new school. Toward the end of sixth grade, some kids had started making fun of us for being best friends because he was a boy and I was a girl. But no matter what changes came, I would never dump my best friend. And he'd never drop me. I hoped. In the meantime, we had the summer and *Monsters Unleashed*.

When the *Monsters Unleashed* game came out a month earlier, its popularity quickly exploded. The first couple of days, it was just the kids and gamers out there playing. Then I saw Mrs. Dorsey, the librarian, playing it in the park. And Old Man Humphrey, whose former favorite hobby was yelling out his front window at any kid who dared poke a toe onto his grass, was caught trespassing in a neighbor's yard to catch a TeddyGlob. Now, instead of yelling at us to stay off his lawn, he yelled things like, "There's a FireWing in the common! Good luck!"

My parents usually nagged me about playing too many video games. "Why don't you and Charlie go for a nature walk? Or ride bikes? When I was your age, I spent all summer riding my bike." But when they were our age, video games were, like, Stone Age quality. No wonder they abandoned their joy sticks to wander outside aimlessly.

Anyway, they didn't complain much about *Monsters Unleashed*. To play, you had to leave your house. The game was about hybrid monsters that were created in a lab. But then they broke out, and players needed to catch them in the "real world." The mobile game used your phone's camera and graphics card to make it look like the monster was really there. You "caught" them by launching BattleNets, which were nets made of "magical material" that could trap a monster and zap it into your phone.

The door slammed behind me as I entered my house. A breeze from the air conditioner hit my face, and it felt so refreshing that I closed my eyes and sighed.

"Bexley?" Mom's voice called out. "Is that you?"

I cringed at the use of my full name. The day I turned eighteen, I swore I was going to legally change it to just Bex. I turned the corner into the kitchen and inhaled deeply. *Mmm*, cookies. Was there any better smell in the world?

Mom was sitting at the kitchen island, squinting at her laptop.

I grabbed a warm cookie and said, "You know, your glasses work better when you put them in front of your eyes."

"I lost them again," Mom said absentmindedly as she scrolled.

I did one of those fake coughs into my hand.

Mom looked up. "What?"

I pointed to the top of her head. She patted her wavy brown-and-gray hair and laughed as she felt the wire-rimmed glasses perched on top. "Thanks, honey."

"No problem, genius." The joke was, my mom was kind of a genius. She'd started her own online business selling personalized jewelry out of the house. And it had grown a ton this year, increasing sales month after month. But, while she ran a business entirely by herself, sometimes the little things slipped by her. Like losing her glasses when they were on top of her head.

"Charlie's coming over in a minute," I said between bites of cookie.

Her eyes had returned to her computer screen. "He can stay for dinner if he'd like. I have a lasagna in the oven."

My parents were pretty cool about Charlie coming over a lot. Mostly because he was my best friend, but also because they knew how miserable things were for him next door with his bully of a brother.

The front door opened and shut, and a voice called out, "Yes! Air conditioning!"

Charlie came strutting into the kitchen, his blonde hair flopping into his eyes. He wore a gray

T-shirt with the NASA logo on it because it wasn't enough to be nerdy; he had to advertise it as well.

He immediately grabbed a cookie and moaned after his first bite. "This cookie is incredible, Mrs. Grayson. When you're done conquering the jewelry world, you should start another business selling these."

"Maybe I will, Charlie!" Mom beamed. "But in the meantime, I have to take a conference call in my office." She pointed at the oven. "When that beeps, take the lasagna out."

"*Mmm*, lasagna," Charlie said dreamily.

"Yes, you're invited," I said.

"Mrs. Grayson, you're the best!" he called out.

Mom waved over her shoulder as she carried her laptop out of the room.

Once she was gone, Charlie slid into a chair and did a little drumroll with his hands on the island countertop. "So I've been thinking about your problem."

I poured us a couple glasses of lemonade. "Which problem is that?"

"I know; there are so many." He smirked. "The *Monsters Unleashed* one. How you're sick of catching the common monsters and want to find the rare ones. And that theory you came up with."

"That monsters like to hang out in old places with a lot of history?"

"Yeah. I think we proved that idea true when we found the VampWolf outside that church downtown. But we already hit up the obvious old places—the town hall, the churches."

I took a long sip of lemonade. "Exactly. We need to know where else in town is old or historically significant."

Charlie wagged his eyebrows up and down.

I giggled. "I smell an idea brewing. Like, literally, I think there's smoke coming from your ears."

He punched me lightly on the arm. "So my grandfather has all this old stuff in his attic. Sometimes I spend the day at his house if you're busy or, well, whatever. But one time when I was up in his attic I saw this map."

I sat up straighter in my seat. "What kind of map?"

"It was a map of town, but it was from the 1800s."

My pulse sped up as I realized where he was going with this. "So everything on that map that still exists today would be really old!"

Charlie nodded. "We could find where the monsters are hiding. The cool, rare monsters."

I clapped my hands together excitedly. "Would your grandfather be up for two visitors tonight?"

Charlie smiled, his braces gleaming, and motioned at the plate in front of us. "As long as we bring him some of these cookies."

After dinner, Charlie and I headed out to his grandfather's house. I held a foil-covered paper plate full of cookies in one hand and my phone in the other. Grandpa Tepper lived on the other side of the town common. And if we had to walk through it anyway, I figured I might as well see if there were any monsters around. The sun was setting, and different monsters came out at night.

"How do you know the moon is going broke?" Charlie asked.

I gave him a look. I was not in the mood for one of his science jokes.

"C'mon." He elbowed me lightly in the side. "How do you know the moon is going broke?"

With a sigh, I said, "I don't know. How?"

"It's down to its last quarter!"

He laughed like it was the funniest joke in the world. I ended up joining in. Not because I liked it, or any of his science jokes, but because Charlie's laugh was kind of contagious.

Finally, we reached the town common. It was an open, grassy area where people could picnic or throw a Frisbee around on a nice day. There was a white gazebo in the center, next to a statue of John Wolcott, the founder of Wolcott, Massachusetts. I'd caught an OinkCat at that statue once that had earned me one hundred experience points!

I was hoping to catch another monster now, but as we neared the gazebo, I froze. Someone else was hanging out by the statue.

Someone I really didn't want to see.

2

wrung my hands nervously while my stomach threatened to do a hard reboot.

Charlie, who'd been walking one step behind me, bumped into my back. "What's going on?"

I pulled him behind the nearest tree, then pointed at my enemy. Willa Tanaka. Ugh. If she were a monster, she'd be called Backstabby, and her defensive power would be throwing knives at your shoulder blades when you thought she was your friend.

As if he were reading my mind, Charlie whispered, "Remember when you guys were friends?"

I rolled my eyes. "That was, like, third grade." Actually it was second through fifth grade. Until Willa realized she was super pretty and thought that gave her a license to act ugly.

"Why are we hiding?" Charlie asked.

"Because I don't feel like being insulted by her right now."

"You know you can't hide from her when school starts back up again."

"Why not? I could probably fit in my locker."

He gave me a look. "Bex . . ."

"Okay, I'll stand up to Willa when you stand up to your brother."

Charlie exhaled loudly. "Point taken."

I didn't know why Willa had been hanging out around the statue all alone, but she had to have moved on by now. I poked my head around the tree. She was still there. And she saw me. Busted.

"What do we have here?" Willa put one hand on her hip, and an evil smile spread slowly across her face. "It's Charlie Tepp-nerd and the ballet-school dropout."

First, it wasn't ballet *school*. It was a class. And,

yes, I quit it. But not because I was terrible. I wasn't great either, don't get me wrong. I quit because I didn't want to deal with Willa's comments anymore.

You call that a tendu? *More like a ten-don't!*

Poor Bexley. Her IQ is lower than her relevé.

Even though other girls in class had been cool and had said nice things, at night when I tried to sleep it was only Willa's insults bouncing around in my head. It got to the point where I didn't enjoy dance anymore. Even on days when Willa wasn't there, I could still hear her making fun of me.

That was part of why I liked *Monsters Unleashed* so much. I was actually good at it. No, I was great. Not that I was horrible at everything else; but it seemed like anything I tried, I was just okay at. I was in the school band but only played the triangle. I wasn't picked last in gym class but was far from first. I was always the middle of the pack in everything. But with *Monsters Unleashed*, I was the best.

It was too bad Willa wasn't a monster. I'd toss a BattleNet at her head so fast she wouldn't even see it coming.

"Go away, Willa," Charlie said, stepping in front of me.

"Why? So you guys can nerd out in private? What are you doing? Playing that stupid game again?"

I hated that I got so tongue-tied in front of her. Any time she lobbed one of her insults, I froze like a helpless Zebot on Hypnosis Tonic. Of course, five minutes after she walked away, I would always think of the best comebacks of all time. But in the moment, my brain was as useful as a pile of dirt.

Willa clucked her tongue. "Nothing to say, huh, Bex? You're such a loser, you almost make it too easy." She shook her head in fake pity, tossed her long, perfectly shiny, black hair over her shoulder, and sauntered off.

I blinked quickly, willing my eyes to dry. Don't cry. Don't let her get to you.

"Are you okay?" Charlie asked softly.

"Yeah, sure." I shrugged. "Just Willa being Willa."

Willa cast one last look over her shoulder and I thought I saw something—regret?—flash on her face, but she was too far away to really tell.

"Let's go," Charlie said. "Before I change my mind and keep all those cookies for myself."

A few minutes later we were inside Grandpa Tepper's old white house. The outside needed a paint job and the inside needed an everything job. Each room had wallpaper that out-weirded the previous room's. And the kitchen had roosters everywhere— from the walls, to the oven mitts, to the tiles on the countertops.

"Somebody really likes roosters," I whispered to Charlie as his grandfather inspected our offering of cookies.

"It was my grandma," Charlie whispered back. "Grandpa hates the roosters, but he doesn't want to change anything from the way she had it when she was alive."

I cringed. Presenting . . . Bexley Grayson, the worst person in the world!

Charlie pled our case and handed over the bribe of fresh-baked cookies.

"So what do you think, Grandpa?" he asked. "Can we go upstairs and look at your old map?"

Grandpa Tepper narrowed his eyes at us. "You can look at it. But you can't have it. And don't smudge it with your dirty fingers."

"We'll only take pictures of it with Bex's phone," Charlie promised.

"Fine," he grunted. "I'm going to put together a

tub of homemade sauce for you to bring home to your mother."

"Thanks, Grandpa!" Charlie took me by the arm and pulled me out of the kitchen. "Quick, before he changes his mind. He can be very possessive about the stuff in his attic."

I followed Charlie to the second floor. He pulled on a chain in the ceiling, and a panel came down with a wooden ladder that folded out.

Charlie motioned with his hand. "Ladies first."

I peered up the steps at the completely dark attic. "Nah, that's cool. You can go."

With a grin, Charlie turned and climbed up the steps. I followed closely behind. The attic smelled musty and gross, and I had that feeling in my nose like I had to sneeze, but it just wouldn't come.

Charlie pulled on a string, and a bare light bulb lit up the room. The attic was bigger than I was expecting and packed wall-to-wall with boxes and stuff. The attic in my house was tiny and only fit our Christmas decorations. I didn't even know how we'd begin to search.

"Do you remember where the map is?" I asked hopefully. I didn't want to spend all night here.

"I think it was in that corner," Charlie said, pointing and heading over.

Oh, yeah? I see you're here in the common with all of your friends! Get it? Because you're ALONE?

Right on schedule, my brain had come up with a good comeback to Willa, who was nowhere around. I sighed. It *was* strange that she had been hanging around the common all by herself. But I had other priorities at the moment.

"Hey, do you know your grandpa's Wi-Fi password?" I wanted to open the *Monsters Unleashed* app to check if there was any activity in the house. I liked to connect to Wi-Fi anytime I could to save my data for when I needed it.

Charlie took the top off a box and coughed as a cloud of dust rose into his face. "Yeah, it's 'countersign.'"

"Countersign?" I repeated.

"Yeah, it's a military term. Grandpa fought in the Vietnam War." Charlie searched through the box and then put the top back on. "Speaking of which, don't touch any of his medals or war stuff."

"I won't." I was too busy scanning the area for monsters. So far, nothing, but this was an old house. So who knew what would pop up?

Charlie opened the top to the next box and then whooped. "Found it!"

"Yes!" I rushed to his side and peered over his shoulder.

The map was old, all right. The paper was yellowed and curled at the edges. It looked so thin, I was scared that it would fall apart if we touched it. Charlie laid it on top of a box and smoothed it out.

"Careful," I said. I didn't want it to rip. Grandpa Tepper would rip our heads off. "Where did he get this, anyway?"

"Who knows? It could've been passed down in the family. But he and Grandma used to love to shop at yard sales and antique stores, so they might have bought it, too."

"Couldn't you just ask him?"

Charlie chewed on his fingernail. "He's having trouble remembering things lately."

I looked down. "Oh."

"Okay, take your pictures," Charlie said. "I'm going to explore a bit. I haven't been up here in a while."

I snapped one big photo, then leaned closer to zoom in and took several photos of each area of the map. The date in the corner was 1856. There wasn't much to Wolcott back then. The fire station was in the same place. St. Bridget's Church still stood on the corner near the common. But most of the other buildings and landmarks were unknown to me. I was going to have so much fun figuring out this map!

Charlie's voice echoed from the other side of the attic. "He has some cool old machines up here."

I smiled to myself. Charlie was the most curious person I knew. He was definitely going to be some kind of scientist someday. Hopefully not a mad scientist, although he sure looked like one when he wore those big protective goggles for chemistry experiments in his basement.

And me? I wanted to be a programmer. I wanted to create apps that improved people's lives and games that made them happy. Only two more years and I could start to take programming electives in high school. But first I had to survive middle school.

"Huh," I heard Charlie say from across the attic. "I wonder what this does."

I heard the metallic flick of a switch, then a sparking noise, and Charlie yelped like a dog. I put the map back in the box and darted over.

"What happened?"

"Ouch, ouch, ouch." Charlie waved his hand in the air. "I turned on that machine and it burned my finger."

Machine? What machine? I nudged Charlie aside and gazed at the contraption atop the table behind him. I'd never seen anything like it. The machine was dark green with several dials and switches. It was rusty in spots and any words that had once been painted on it had since been rubbed off.

I put my hands on my hips. "Weren't you the one telling me not to touch any of your Grandpa's stuff?"

He blushed. "Yeah. And I'm pretty sure I fried the thing. Let's get out of here before I cause any more trouble."

"Okay, I just want to make sure my pictures came out clear." I squinted at my phone in the dim light and swiped through my photo gallery. They all looked good. I couldn't wait to get home and examine them.

I closed my photo gallery and the *Monsters Unleashed* app that had been running in the background popped back up. I noticed that the Wi-Fi was down, probably from the electrical surge that the dumb machine had zapped out. But something else looked strange, too. My brows drew together.

"What's wrong?" Charlie asked.

"Wait . . ." It couldn't be. I probably just needed to reload it. I closed the app, made sure I was connected to cellular data, and opened it again. But the results were the same. "Oh, no. OH, NO!"

I turned the phone around to show Charlie.

His eyes bugged out of his head. "Um, . . . why is your Monster Lab empty? Where are all of your monsters?"

"They're gone!" I shrieked.

Charlie put his hands on my shoulders. "Okay, calm down. Stop screaming. I don't want my Grandpa to know I touched any of his stuff."

"What about *my* stuff?!" My heart pounded loudly in my ears. "I think when you turned that machine on, it killed the Wi-Fi, and somehow emptied my Monster Lab!"

"This makes no sense." Charlie dragged his fingers through his already messy hair. "Let's leave and try again. Maybe it needs to reload outside of the house."

Charlie said his good-byes to his grandfather, and we left with a Tupperware container of homemade spaghetti sauce. I don't know how much garlic people usually put in their sauce, but based on the smell,

I estimated that Grandpa Tepper's had 10,000 times more garlic.

I could only manage a small wave good-bye as we stepped off the porch. I'd spent weeks catching monsters, trading in the ones worth less to power up the better ones, and cultivating my Monster Lab. I'd had ten powerful beasts in there. It would take me ages to build them back up again. It wasn't a matter of just catching ten more. I'd caught hundreds and transferred them to earn monster points that gave my best ones power-ups. Some people played for quantity. I played for quality. I was proud of the ten monsters I'd had. And now they were all gone.

The night air was just as hot and humid as the afternoon had been. Grandpa Tepper's road was dark and deserted. Much like my empty Monster Lab.

"Okay, try again," Charlie insisted.

I pressed on the app and opened the Lab. My stomach sank into my feet. Still empty. My monsters were gone.

"Let's . . . um . . . let's start walking home," Charlie said. Because what else could he say? He'd played around with a machine he had no business touching, and it had ruined my game.

I kicked at a pebble. "I can't believe I lost everything. Everything!"

"Well, we have the map now," Charlie said sheepishly.

"Which is handy since I have to start all over!" I shook my head. "I don't understand what happened. How could all ten monsters disappear from my Monster Lab? Where did they go? Did that stupid machine zap them somewhere? Like, to someone else's phone?"

Charlie shrugged. "I don't know, Bex. It's a game. Games glitch out. And I'm sorry, but we're not going to solve it right now."

He sounded sad, and I knew he felt guilty. It wasn't his fault. He didn't know that the machine would ruin everything. I inhaled a deep breath and let it out. I felt myself calming down a little.

"Yeah, you're right. I'll start fresh tomorrow."

We cut through the common, past the gazebo and the statue, which looked lonely in the empty night. I wanted to get home as quickly as possible and throw myself into bed. Tomorrow was a new day, but this one was a nightmare.

"Let's take Nightshade." I pointed at the gloomy

side road. It had only one street light and a couple houses. Main Street was brighter and decidedly less creepy, but cutting through Nightshade Road would be quicker.

Charlie looked unsure but agreed.

We shuffled along in near silence, the only noise the echoing of our own footsteps. I stewed about my gaming loss. Charlie was probably worrying about his Grandpa finding out about the fried machine. But he'd be fine. That machine obviously hadn't been touched in decades. And it was clear it should never be used again!

A rustling came from the bushes farther down the road.

"Did you hear that?" Charlie whispered.

"Yeah. Probably a rabbit or something."

The noise came again, slightly louder and closer this time. Goose bumps rose on my arms despite the muggy heat. The street lamp above us flickered.

"This is starting to get creepy," Charlie said.

I looked up at the orange bulb just in time to see it spark and go dead, draping us in darkness.

Charlie grabbed my arm. "I have upgraded the situation to Definitely, Officially Creepy."

I pressed the HOME button on my phone, and the screen lit up. It cast a bluish glow, but only reached a couple of feet in front of us. Beyond that lay darkness, and who knew what else. I turned on my flashlight app and aimed it at the gloom.

A low growl came from not too far away. It was a unique sound I would have recognized anywhere. But it wasn't an angry dog growl. That would have been better.

"You know that sound, right?" Charlie's trembling voice asked.

I swallowed hard. "Yeah. It's a VampWolf."

3

he monster emerged from behind a tree. It was covered in fur, like a wolf, but also had two long, sharp fangs poking out of its mouth, and glowing red eyes. The VampWolf was the perfect combination of horrifying and terrifying. It was *torrifying*. I didn't even care that wasn't a word. I was so scared, I needed a *new* word.

"Are you seeing what I'm seeing?" I asked Charlie.

"If you're seeing an actual VampWolf walking toward us, then yes."

"How can this be happening?" I looked down at my phone. The *Monsters Unleashed* app wasn't even open. I wasn't looking through the screen. The monster was really there, in the middle of the street.

This wasn't a game. The VampWolf was right there in front of us on the street.

"Maybe it will run away," Charlie said.

The VampWolf lurched forward, eyes narrowed, teeth bared.

"Or not," I said.

I wanted to run, but my legs wouldn't move. And it probably wasn't a bright idea. The VampWolf had a maximum-speed stat. It could outrun us easily. Our only chance was a defensive tactic. But we didn't have any weapons. Or did we . . .

"Throw the sauce," I whispered.

"What?" Charlie replied, shaking like a bowl of Jell-O.

"The spaghetti sauce," I said between gritted teeth. "It has a lot of garlic."

Charlie's eyes widened as he picked up on my meaning. The VampWolf was known for its hatred of garlic.

The VampWolf took another step, so close now that I could see its red eyes flare.

Charlie fumbled with the container, trying to pry the top off.

"Hurry!" I screeched.

Closer now, the VampWolf snarled and flashed its teeth. I recognized that move. It was a warning. Its next move would be a full attack. It hissed, opened its mouth . . . and Charlie tossed the entire container of spaghetti sauce with extra garlic into it.

"Nice shot!" I yelled.

The VampWolf let out an eardrum-shattering shriek. Then it bent over and retched onto the road. Was this really happening? Was I watching a monster barf?

"Time to go!" Charlie grabbed my arm and pulled me away.

I didn't need much convincing. I tore into the fastest run my legs had ever accomplished in my life, careening around corners, jumping over curbs, until we were finally back on our own road.

I bent over, heaving and trying to catch my breath.

Charlie's face was as pale as the moon. "How am I going to explain losing the spaghetti sauce?"

A laugh escaped from my throat. "Not really important right now. I'm more focused on how we just saw a real VampWolf."

Charlie shrugged and put his hands in the pockets of his shorts. "I wasn't scared."

I rolled my eyes at him. "Yeah, just like when you say, 'I'm not cold' on winter mornings when you refuse to wear a coat to the bus stop, but you're shaking from your head to your feet."

He threw his hands up. "Okay, fine. I was scared. You were, too!"

"Of course I was! We saw a VampWolf in real life." I paused because that sounded so crazy. "We did, right? I didn't dream the whole thing?"

Charlie reached over and pinched my arm.

I slapped his hand. "Ouch!"

"Well, now we know we're not dreaming."

I groaned. "So what should we do?"

Charlie looked around fearfully. "Probably head inside and talk about it in the morning."

He was right. Just because we were steps away from our houses didn't mean we were safe. The VampWolf could have followed us. It could be hiding in any bush, behind any tree. I shuddered.

"See you tomorrow," I said quickly and ran up the steps to my house.

After a pleasant night of nonstop nightmares, I woke up feeling crabby and tired. I immediately made plans to hide in my room all day. Then there was a knock on the door.

"Come in," I called.

Mom entered and wrinkled her nose like she did when my room was messy.

"I'll clean it," I said quickly. "That's my plan for the whole day, actually. This is going to be the clean-est room in the house."

Mom's eyebrows rose halfway up her forehead. "That's . . . nice, Bexley. But before you begin, isn't there something you forgot?"

I tried to use my brain but all it could recall were the VampWolf's red eyes. "Um, breakfast?"

Mom sighed. "You told Mrs. Sweeney that you'd walk William Shakespaw while they were away for the weekend."

Yup. William Shakespaw. That's what happens when an English teacher gets a dog. And why had I agreed to walk him? Oh, ten dollars. That was why.

But no amount of money was worth leaving the house right now.

What was my other choice, though? To tell my mom, *I'm pretty sure I saw a VampWolf last night, so I have no need to leave the house this morning. Or ever again.*

Instead I slapped on a fake smile and said, "I'll go walk him right now."

"Don't forget sunscreen!" Mom called.

I went into the bathroom and lathered SPF 50 on my pale, freckled face. If they sold SPF 2000, I'd use that. I'd been sunburned badly only once, and it was an experience I'd rather not re-create. I'd spent the night in bed shivering, trying not to vomit, and not moving because even my soft sheets felt like razor blades against my skin. Not a good look. Ever since, it had become Mom's number one mission in life to remind me about sunscreen whenever I went outside.

I tied my sneakers and headed out the front door into the deceptively beautiful sunny day. The sky was a cloudless blue, and the birds were chirping loudly. But there was also a monster out there somewhere, and that took some of the shine off the whole thing.

The Sweeneys lived on the other side of the Teppers, only a few hundred feet away. But the walk felt like hours, and I spent most of it looking over my shoulder. I took the key they kept hidden under the potted plant on the porch and let myself in, breathing a sigh of relief as I closed the door behind me. Safe again. For now.

"William Shakespaw!" I yelled. "Where are you?"

I heard him before I saw him, the tags on his collar doing that jingle-jangle his whole way into the front hall. When he saw me, his tail started wagging. He was a cute little dude. But if we ran into a monster on our walk, the white puffball known as William Shakespaw wasn't going to save me. He was 16 years old, which is 112 in dog years. And he weighed 20 pounds.

I scratched him behind the ear. "Who's a good boy? Is it you?"

He pushed himself against my leg and licked my hand.

"I'm sorry, pal, but this is going to be your shortest walk ever. Very disappointing. I apologize in advance."

I clipped the leash onto his collar and, with one last look out the window, brought us outside. William trotted happily beside me as I led us toward the cul-de-sac at the end of the road. He stopped to do the first part of his business at a fire hydrant and two trees, but he still hadn't done the other part. The longer we stayed outside, the more nervous and impatient I felt.

We reached the end of the road where a cul-de-sac circled two houses with a section of woods in between. I got a bad feeling when I stared into the woods—like the woods were staring back.

Stop, I told myself. *You're working yourself up for no reason.*

William let out a low growl. Okay, maybe now there was a reason. In all the years I'd known that happy little dog, I'd heard him growl exactly zero times.

"What is it, boy?"

He stiffened and bared his teeth. His normally wagging tail was pointed down, between his legs. He stared at the woods for a moment longer, then huffed and continued walking.

That was weird. But it didn't mean he'd seen or smelled a monster. He was a dog. It could've just been a squirrel or something.

William stopped in front of a little yellow house and began circling and sniffing.

I rolled my eyes. "Just poop already. There's no need to make a big production out of it."

He got into position, and I looked away to give him some privacy. That's when I noticed the road had gotten quiet. Like eerily quiet. The birds had stopped chirping. They'd been so loud when I'd left the house. Why would all the birds in the area suddenly go silent or take off?

A sense of dread grew in my belly.

William finished, and I quickly picked it up with a poop bag.

"Time to go," I said. "Like really fast."

I tried to jog, but the little guy wasn't so speedy in his old age. So I picked him up and carried him in my arms. "Sorry, bud. Worst walk ever. I know."

I couldn't shake the feeling that someone was watching me. When I looked over my shoulder, I thought I saw a flash of something white dart behind a tree, but it could have been my imagination. And the VampWolf wasn't white, so that was good. I put William Shakespaw back in his house, tossed the poop bag in the trash, and replaced their key.

By the time I reached my front yard, I was so relieved that I'd begun to whistle. No VampWolf had attacked me. Maybe the whole thing was over. I pulled my phone out of my pocket and opened the *Monsters Unleashed* app, hope soaring in my chest. But my shoulders sagged as I saw that my Monster Lab was still empty.

And then my heart stopped.

A gurgling sound came from behind me. I twirled around and found myself facing a Uniguin. The half-penguin, half-unicorn, all-angry monster that I'd caught on my phone yesterday was standing on my front lawn. It was almost cute, with its short legs and round tummy. But then it opened its mouth, and I remembered that Uniguins had fangs.

And I had no garlic to save me this time. Not that Uniguins minded garlic. In fact, they had no specific, secret weakness. They were just easy to catch. In the game, anyway. How on earth was I supposed to catch one in real life?

It gurgled again and stepped a bit closer, like it was curious about me. Or maybe wanted to bite me. I didn't really know and didn't want to find out. But the Uniguin stood between my house and me, so I couldn't make a run for the front door.

My mother's face popped up in the window behind

the Uniguin, watching. I didn't know why she was just standing there staring. Why wasn't she running out to save me? Was she in shock?

My phone nearly slipped out of my suddenly sweaty hand. I stared down at it, at the open *Monsters Unleashed* app. And I decided to do the only thing I knew how to do. Battle.

I aimed my phone at the Uniguin while it cocked its head like a curious puppy. Usually I saw the monster through my phone's camera only. It was strange to see it on the screen *and* in the real world behind the phone. I swiped my finger and launched a Battle-Net on the screen. It missed the Uniguin by an inch, coming close enough to make it duck its head. My pulse sped up. The BattleNet on the screen had affected the monster in real life!

And it did not like that.

It snarled at me, stepping closer, saliva dripping from its fangs.

Mom still stood in the window, motionless, like she was watching me sniff flowers or something.

I launched another BattleNet. The monster ducked, squatting on its short legs.

The screen door opened behind it, and Mom

popped her head out. "Bexley, I know you love that mindless game, but you can't spend your whole summer playing it."

Um, what? Doesn't she see that I am battling for my life?

Mom crossed her arms over her chest. "Don't ignore me when I'm talking to you."

"One sec, Mom!" *Just saving our lives here! No big deal! Can't she see that?*

I launched two more BattleNets in quick succession, one aimed left and one right. The Uniguin lurched forward, so close that I could smell it—a combination of wet dog and four-day-old burrito. And finally, the second BattleNet was a direct hit. There was a zap, a flash of light, and my phone buzzed in my hands.

The Uniguin had been right in front of me. Like a foot away. And now it was gone.

I raised the phone to my eyes. My trembling finger selected the Monster Lab. And there it was—one Uniguin.

I'd caught it in the real world and trapped it back into the game.

Mom sighed. "I appreciate that you're walking

outside and getting exercise, but I worry that while you're staring at your phone, you're missing the real world."

The real world was trying to kill me just now!

But the monster was gone. I'd won the battle. Just like in the game.

Mom gave me a strange look. "Why are you breathing so heavily?"

I pointed at the now empty space in front of me. "You . . . you didn't see that?"

"See what?"

My mind whirred. She hadn't seen the monster, even though it had been right in front of her. And if I told her, she'd think I was crazy and take away my game and my phone for good.

"A mouse," I blurted. "There was a little mouse."

Mom laughed heartily. "That explains it. No wonder you looked so scared. You never were a fan of little furry things."

I pressed a hand against my chest to calm my heart. "Yeah, totally."

"I'm heading back in. The television was flickering. I'm wondering if I need to call a repairman." She turned and went back into the house.

I stood on the lawn, my mind running in circles. Okay, think. Why didn't Mom see the monster? Charlie and I had figured out that we weren't dreaming. But what if that was part of the dream? What if I was still dreaming now? Maybe I was really sick in bed with a fever. One time when I had the flu, I dreamed I was a fire hose, but I'd really just puked all over my bed.

Or maybe I was crazy. That was also a possibility.

"Hey!" Charlie called, darting out of his house toward me. "Did that just happen?"

"Did I get cornered by a real-life Uniguin and battle him back into my Monster Lab? Yes."

Charlie's jaw dropped wider than a SharkFace's. "I saw the end of your fight from my bedroom window. I ran downstairs and outside as fast as I could. Where did your mom go? To call the police?"

I swallowed hard. "She didn't see it."

"Um, what?"

"She couldn't see the monster. I was wondering if I'd gone insane, but you saw it, too."

Charlie chewed on his thumbnail. "Maybe we're both insane."

"*Psst!*"

I looked around, confused at where the sudden noise came from.

"*Psst!*"

Charlie pointed. "I think it's Old Man Humphrey."

I looked across the street and saw the man's shadowy form in his front window. He waved us over. Charlie shrugged, and we crossed to his yard. I expected him to come outside to talk to us, but instead he motioned for us to move closer to the open window.

He pressed his face close to the screen and whispered, "I saw a TeddyGlob last night."

Ugh. He only wanted to give us a monster tip. Usually, I appreciated it. But I was kind of busy right now.

"That's great, Old . . . um, I mean, Mr. Humphrey."

"No," he snapped. "Not great. It peed on my lawn."

Charlie and I shared a look. "Like, really?" I asked.

"Yes, *really*. I may be an old man, but I know the difference between a game on my phone-a-ma-jig and a real monster."

Charlie asked, "What did it do after it . . . watered your lawn?"

"It saw my face in the window, and it snarled at me!" He paused and rubbed his white beard. "You kids think I'm losing my marbles, don't ya?"

"No," Charlie said. "We saw it, too."

"Well, not a TeddyGlob," I clarified. "We saw a VampWolf last night, and I caught a Uniguin this morning. A real Uniguin, in the real world. But I battled it and zapped it back into my phone."

Mr. Humphrey's wrinkled eyes blinked slowly. "What do you mean *back* into your phone?"

I grimaced. "It's kind of a long story, but we were in Charlie's grandpa's attic, and Charlie pressed a button on some old machine, and it zapped everything. My Monster Lab was empty. But this morning after I caught the real Uniguin, it was back in my Monster Lab where it was before."

"Did you also have a VampWolf and a TeddyGlob before this machine zapped them out?" he asked.

"Yes," I answered, figuring out where he was going with this. It wasn't any old monsters roaming the town right now. It was my monsters.

"How many did you have in total?" Mr. Humphrey asked.

"Ten."

He nodded slowly, taking it in. "One down. Nine to go. We need to alert the authorities. We'll show them—"

"Nope," Charlie interrupted. "Bex's mom couldn't see a monster even though it was standing right in front of her."

Old Man Humphrey rubbed his beard again, like he was thinking hard. "Huh. We must be able to see them because we played the game so much that our brain forged the neural pathways."

"The what?" Charlie asked.

"Neuroplasticity!" he said with irritation. "You think you're the only one who knows about science, kid? I was a neuroscientist back in my day, and a good one at that. I know a thing or two."

"Then what do we do now?" I asked. "Nine of my monsters are still out there."

Mr. Humphrey let out a heavy sigh. "A great responsibility has landed in your laps. I'm no help. I can't walk to my mailbox without getting a leg cramp. Most people in town won't be able to see the monsters. And they won't believe you."

"So it's up to us," I said slowly.

With his face still pressed against the window screen, Mr. Humphrey spoke with determination. "You have to catch those monsters before they start hurting people."

He was right. It was *my* Lab that got emptied into the world. They were my monsters. It was my responsibility to catch them before they harmed anyone. Charlie would help me. Maybe we'd find others, too, who would join our search.

I only hoped we could do it without becoming monster lunch ourselves.

printed out the photographs of the map I'd taken with my phone and spread them across the desk in my room.

Charlie let out a dramatic sigh. "Where do we even start?"

"Don't get overwhelmed," I said to both him and myself. "Let's inspect the map first and see what we learn."

We didn't want to wander around town with no plan, so we decided to do our monster hunting where they'd most likely be—the oldest places in town. The day had turned into another summer steamer, and I had to turn the fan in my room on high. I placed pens and erasers around the edges of the printed photos so they wouldn't blow away. We both leaned close to them and squinted.

Wolcott was a small town to begin with, but in 1856 it was minuscule. The common was the heart of town, and roads and neighborhoods radiated out from the middle. Now it made sense to me why the houses closer to the town center were old. As the town grew, more streets were added. So the farther out you went, the newer the houses were. This narrowed down a bit the area where the monsters might be.

"Here's our road." Charlie pressed a finger onto the map. "And Grandpa's. And . . . Nightshade." He frowned. "What's that?"

The map showed a building named "Meeting House." But that building wasn't at the end of Nightshade Road anymore. I vaguely remembered seeing some kind of historical marker there, though, with a little plaque that said something about a fire.

"That building doesn't exist anymore," I said. "But that explains why the VampWolf was hanging out there. It's a historical site."

Charlie swallowed hard. "Should we . . . go there now and capture it?"

I shook my head. "VampWolves only come out at night, remember?"

"Oh, yeah," he said, sounding relieved.

We would have to track it down eventually, though. But I tried not to think about that at the moment.

"So where should we monster hunt first?" he asked.

My eyes explored the map and landed on a place we knew well. "North Elementary."

"Our school was around in 1856?"

"It looks like it was the one and only school in town back then."

Charlie grimaced. "Which explains why it's the oldest and grossest."

It was true. Our years at North Elementary were fun, but first of all, they lacked air conditioning. Even with a few additions to the original building, it was still too small for the number of students. And it had this weird basement smell most of the time. I may have been worried about starting seventh grade, but at least the middle school building was built fairly recently.

"Should we head out?" I asked. Part of me hoped Charlie would come up with some excuse to procrastinate.

"Maybe we should call around and see if anyone can help us."

That was actually a great idea. I tapped on my chin as I thought. "Hmm . . . who do we know who definitely plays the game?"

"Old Man Humphrey. But he already said he can't help."

"What about Isaac?" I asked. Isaac was not only awesome at the game, he was one of the nicest kids I knew. He'd definitely help us.

Charlie shook his head. "This is the week he's away at camp with some of his friends who also have autism."

He was right. Isaac was really looking forward to this camp. We couldn't call him. "What about Riya?"

"She's away at some science camp."

I sighed. *Dang.* Then I started to rattle off more names. "Andy Badger."

"Boy Scout camping trip."

"Steve Pak."

"Baseball camp."

I threw my hands up. "Is everyone at camp? Jeez!"

"What about Marcus Moore?" Charlie suggested.

Marcus was one grade above us, but well known in our *Monsters Unleashed* community. He had awesome monsters, high scores. Almost as high as mine. If anyone could help us, it would be him. But he was a little . . . intimidating. His gaming skills had given him an ego the size of the Cloud. He was also totally cute, and I'd had a crush on him for a long time, so that made me mega-nervous.

"I don't have his number," I said.

"Yeah, you do. Remember there was that group text about the video-game animation class? He was on it."

Oh, yeah. I did have his number. And now I had no excuse.

I scrolled through my contacts until I found Marcus's name. I hit the CALL button. Then, in a brilliant move, I handed the phone to the Charlie.

"What?" His eyes bugged out of his head. "I'm not talking to him. You talk to him!"

"I'm not talking to him!"

"It's your phone!"

"It was your idea!"

We continued to toss the phone back and forth like a hot potato until we heard a tiny third voice.

"One of you had better talk to me because this is getting boring."

Gulp. I slowly put the phone up to my ear. And I tried not to think about his dreamy hazel eyes and how when he smiled, dimples formed in his dark brown skin. "Um, Marcus? This is, um, Bex Grayson."

"Yeah, I know," he said flatly. "Your name flashed on my screen. Technology. Crazy how it works."

I rolled my eyes at his sarcasm. This was nuts. There was no reason to be nervous talking to Marcus. I gave myself a quick, silent pep talk. *Don't think of him as Marcus, totally adorable older boy who's impressively amazing at gaming. Think of him as merely a fellow human in a war against monsters.* I had to get over my useless nerves and get on with it.

I cleared my throat. "Have you . . . seen anything weird around town today? Or yesterday?"

"I'm kind of busy. Can you just get to the point?"

"Monsters!" I blurted. "Are you seeing the monsters?"

He groaned. "Do you have a question about the game or something?"

My stomach rolled over. He hadn't seen them. I would have to explain it all. He probably wouldn't even believe me. But I had to try. "So, listen. Charlie and I were in his grandfather's attic playing with some old technology we shouldn't have been touching, and it crossed some wires, and now the monsters from my Lab are out in the world. Like, the *real* monsters are out there. And only people who've played the game can see them and capture them. So we were hoping you would work with us to, um, do that."

I took a breath and waited through the longest pause in the history of the world. All I heard was some rhythmic sound in the background. It was familiar, but I was so nervous I couldn't place it.

Finally, he spoke. "You two do realize that prank phone calls usually involve anonymity?"

"It's not a prank, Marcus. This is real." Maybe appealing to his ego would work. "We need you. You're the best player in town. We need your skills. We—"

He interrupted, "Listen. I don't know what you're trying to pull, but I'm not going to believe that there are real monsters roaming the streets of town."

"There are!" I screeched. "Just go outside and walk around. You'll see. Go downtown, where the old buildings are. Just do it now and then call me back."

"I can't walk around town right now."

Oh my gosh. I was going to kick his butt. "Why?"

"Because I'm away on vacation with my family."

My head fell forward. That was the rhythmic sound in the background. Ocean waves. "You're at the beach."

"Yeah. And when you two finish with your prank or your hallucination or whatever this is, you should convince your parents to take you down to the shore. There are SharkFaces everywhere. It's awesome. In fact, here's another one. I have to catch it. Later."

The call ended, and I held the silent phone in my hand. I'd always wanted Marcus to notice me, but not this way.

"That went well," Charlie said.

My eyes snapped to his. "You think you could have done better?"

He held his hands up. "Nope! Sorry."

I exhaled loudly. "We can't sit around here all day while the monsters are out there. We have to get started. We'll just have to go it alone."

Charlie straightened his shoulders. "Let's do it. North Elementary—and whatever monster waits inside—here we come!"

"Not so fast," I said. "We need to stop at your house first so you can borrow your mom's phone."

The enthusiasm drained out of him like a leaking balloon. "Do we, though? I mean, she's probably going to say no. And my brother has a friend over."

"I don't know what's waiting for us out there. And, sure, I caught the Uniguin on my own, but the others won't be as easy. Battles are always more successful if you go into them as a team."

His shoulders sagged. "Fine. Let's go ask."

We headed outside and snuck in the side door that led to Charlie's kitchen, carefully avoiding the driveway where Jason and his friend were playing basketball. Jason was only two years older than Charlie but he was built like a three-story house. The puberty train had made an early stop at the Tepper place for Jason many years ago and sort of forgot to come back for Charlie.

Mrs. Tepper was sorting through the mail when we bounded in. She wasn't wearing her scrubs, which meant she wasn't heading out to work anytime soon. That gave Charlie better odds at borrowing her phone. Mrs. Tepper was an ER nurse and sometimes worked crazy hours, but it was pretty handy to have a nurse in the house because Jason got sports injuries, like, every other day.

She looked up at us and smiled. "Hey, you two! How's your day going? Is this weather hot enough for you or what? What are you up to?"

Mrs. Tepper's habit of tossing multiple questions out at once always left me confused. Should I answer them all? In order? Or skip the first few and just answer the last one?

Charlie ignored them all and asked his own. "Can I borrow your phone? Bex and I are going to head out to play the game."

Mrs. Tepper frowned. "Again? When are you going to get sick of that game and move on to something else? Wouldn't you rather stay inside where it's cool and watch some TV?"

Charlie nudged me with his elbow and gave me his *think of something!* face.

"Um," I said. "My mom wants me to play outside. Because it's, um, summer, and, uh, fresh air."

Charlie nodded quickly. I thought it was good.

What self-respecting mother would disagree with fresh air?

She ripped open another envelope and pulled the bill out, halfheartedly inspecting it. "I suppose your mother has a point. I just wish it wasn't necessary to use my phone when you two play outside."

"I wouldn't have to use your phone if you'd let me have my own," Charlie muttered.

"You're not old enough yet."

"Jason was my age when he got a phone."

The kitchen door flew open, and Jason and his friend burst in like a hurricane of sweat and gross.

Jason yelled (he didn't seem to be capable of speaking at normal volume), "I got a phone because I needed to call Mom when practice was over so she could come get me. Where do you need her to pick *you* up from? The only place you go is next door."

"I go lots of places," Charlie insisted. "School, the park, the library, downtown."

Mrs. Tepper ignored the argument. "Would you boys like a drink? Would you like a snack? Would you like some fruit? I have fresh oranges."

She pushed a bowl of oranges toward Jason and his silent friend.

"What do you need Mom's phone for? To play your stupid little game?" Jason taunted.

Charlie crossed his arms. "It's none of your business."

Jason picked up an orange and launched it at Charlie's head. Charlie didn't duck in time and it bounced right off his forehead. He bent down and grabbed it and threw it back at Jason. But he missed, and the weaponized fruit dropped harmlessly to the floor.

Jason rubbed a hand over his buzz cut and sneered, "You throw like a girl."

I wanted to throw the entire bowl—like a girl—straight at his nose. But that wouldn't help the situation. Then he'd just make fun of Charlie for needing a *girl* to stick up for him. One of these days, though. One of these days. I looked at Mrs. Tepper, basically pleading with my eyes for her to do something.

She shrugged. "Boys will be boys. Always teasing each other."

Except it wasn't teasing. And it wasn't both ways. It made me so angry that Jason treated Charlie so badly and their parents did nothing about it. Charlie's mom ignored the problem. And his dad, Jason Sr., agreed with Jason Junior and was always trying to "toughen Charlie up." The whole thing made my head want to explode but also made me glad that I was an only child.

As Jason and his friend walked by, I had to grit my teeth to keep my mouth shut. They went into the living room and turned on the TV. I peeked around the corner and eavesdropped.

The silent friend finally spoke. "Hey, you're kind of hard on your little brother, man."

"He's an embarrassment," Jason scoffed. "I have to give him a hard time. It's my job."

His friend shrugged and began to peel his orange.

"Let's go," Charlie hissed in my ear.

I didn't even hear him sneak up behind me. I looked down at the phone in his hand. "She changed her mind?"

"Yeah. I only have an hour, though." He blushed slightly. "I think she felt bad."

Good, I thought. *She should.*

5

'd spent many years inside the school's walls, but as I cupped my hands around my eyes and peered through a window, it looked creepy. No kids dashing down the hall. No teachers standing in their classrooms. No poor attempts at student artwork hanging on the walls. Just emptiness.

And maybe a monster.

"How are we going to get inside?" Charlie asked.

I pulled back from the window. Honestly, I hadn't

thought that far ahead. Of course, the doors would be locked for the summer.

I scratched at my chin. "Maybe one of these windows is open?"

"You take this side," Charlie said. "I'll go around back."

As Charlie's footsteps faded away, I moved from one window to the next, peeking at each to see if there was an opening at the bottom. But every one was closed.

I met Charlie around the back of the school and heaved a sigh. "None of the windows are open."

"No," Charlie said, grinning. "But this one's unlocked."

I took a closer look at the window behind him. He was right! The window latch was pointing left while all the others pointed right. It was totally unlocked.

We popped the screen out. Charlie grunted, straining to push up the window. Then he motioned with his hand. "Ladies first."

This time I knew he was only offering because he was nervous, but I didn't care. I scrambled up the brick wall and through the window, landing on my feet in a classroom. Charlie came in after me, a little less gracefully.

Even though it was daytime, the school seemed dark and gray. I flipped a switch and long fluorescent bulbs lit up the hallway.

"It smells worse than hydrogen sulfide in here," Charlie said.

I had no idea what that meant, but I agreed. "Where should we look first?"

He thought for a moment. "Maybe the cafeteria? It could be searching for food." His voice did a weird screechy thing, which was either fear- or puberty-related.

"Good plan."

We inched down the hallway, trying to keep our footsteps as muffled as possible.

Charlie whispered, "I've been trying to remember all the monsters that were in your Lab the day they got zapped. You had two Uniguins, a Zebot, an Oink-Cat, and a VampWolf—that's still out there some-where, by the way . . ."

I searched my memory. "I also had a TeddyGlob and a SharkFace."

"Yikes."

"And a FurClaw and a FireWing."

Charlie's eyes widened. "Oh, man. Oh, man. Oh, man. Oh, man!"

I winced, remembering the worst of all. "And . . ."

"And what?" Charlie prodded.

"The other day, when you couldn't borrow your mom's phone, I played the game alone. I didn't mention what I caught because I didn't want you to be sad that I got it without you—"

"What?" Charlie interrupted, raising his voice. "What is it?"

I took a breath. "A SpiderFang."

Charlie stopped walking. Stopped breathing. No sound or movement of any kind came out of him for a long moment. And then he screeched, "There is a REAL LIVE SpiderFang out there?!"

"Well, not right now. They only come out at night."

"Yeah," he yelled, "which means we'll have to go out at night to catch it!"

"Let's just take it one monster at a time," I said, trying to calm him down. "We'll focus on clearing the school first. I mean, there might not even be a monster here right now."

The lights flickered above us.

Charlie grabbed my arm. "Remember when we were on Nightshade Road and the street lamp went out?"

I could tell what he was thinking. "And when the Uniguin was outside of my house, the TV started acting weird. My mom said it was flickering."

"The monsters must affect the electricity around them," Charlie said.

"So one is definitely here."

We gulped simultaneously.

The cafeteria was through the double doors at the end of the hall. I leaned my ear up against one of them and heard nothing. But would I hear something through a metal door? I didn't know.

Charlie had started to bounce in place. "We'll just burst in there, phones blazing. Take it by surprise."

I shrugged. It was as good a plan as any. I held the phone in my sweaty hand and opened the app. My battle weapons were loaded and ready to go. Charlie held his mother's phone in one shaking hand and pushed on the door with the other.

He yelled out in what could only be described as a battle cry and went tearing into the cafeteria, jumping up on a table and turning around 360 degrees. I came in behind him, a bit more reserved, and eyed the corners for any movement.

It was empty. No monsters. And also, no food. So we couldn't even grab a chocolate pudding for our trouble.

"Let's head back into the hall," Charlie said. "Hurry." Beads of sweat dripped down his forehead, and his face was flushed.

I put a hand up. "Hey, slow down. What's the rush?"

"I haven't fought a monster yet like you have. I feel like I'm going to puke, okay? I'm in a rush because I want to get this over with."

He pushed past me into the hall. I tried to keep up, but his longer legs kept him a distance away. He turned the corner toward the art and music hall, and I temporarily lost sight of him. But when I came careening around the corner, I got a face full of his back.

"Why'd you stop?" I asked.

"*Shhh . . .*" He pointed toward the open door halfway down the hall.

I heard the noises first. Slurping, belching, gross noises.

As we got closer, my nostrils flared. The school had never exactly smelled like flowers before, but this stench was nasty. It smelled like a pot full of puke and hot dogs. Not that anyone has ever attempted to cook that combination. It was just the first thing the foul stench brought to mind.

The monster was in the art room. From the sound of it, it was making a giant mess. I carefully peeked my head around the door. Paint was splattered on the floor. Pencils and crayons were strewn about in disarray. And in the middle of it all was an amorphous blob, the color of poop and the smell not too far from it.

A TeddyGlob.

With a burp, it swayed back and forth, rolling this way and that.

Charlie whispered in my ear. "I think it's been sniffing the markers."

TeddyGlobs had the furry heads of teddy bears and the gross bodies of gooey blobs. This one picked up another paint can with its nebulous, gloopy arms and guzzled; then it dropped the can and remaining paint on the ground. If we didn't take care of this soon, the art teacher, Mrs. Micucci, would have no supplies left when school started in September.

In the cafeteria, Charlie had been eager to find the monster right away. But now that it was right in front of us, Charlie made no effort to move.

"Come on," I urged. "Let's do this."

The monster's back was facing us, and it was busy making noises similar to my dad's stomach that night he ate bad fish tacos. We could sneak up and start to battle before it even realized we were here.

"Don't get too close," Charlie whispered.

I took another step. The monster looked soft and mushy, more gross than scary. I'd be fine. But then, almost out of nowhere, a long tendril of yuck—like an arm made of goo—came lashing out of the Teddy-Glob's body and whapped the side of my head. I stumbled into an easel, knocking it over.

I guess it *was* paying attention.

"Are you okay?" Charlie screeched.

"Ugh," I groaned, rubbing my head. "Let's get it."

We aimed our phones and launched simultaneous BattleNets. I thought it would be an easy shot. The TeddyGlob was a big target. But its blob-like nature made it able to duck and swerve in ways that creatures with bones could not.

It rolled and slurped its way toward Charlie. With a yelp of fear, Charlie panicked and walked backward, forgetting to keep, you know, battling. His back hit the wall and he just stood there, frozen.

"Keep going!" I yelled. "Launch another one. We have to do it together."

At my screeching, the TeddyGlob turned its attention toward me.

"Yeah," I said, jutting my chin out. "Come this way, Globby."

I swiped, launching another Net right as Charlie finally launched his. They missed, as the globular monster morphed and dodged them both.

The slurpy beast moved even closer to me, and my heart started to race. I placed my finger on the center of the phone's screen, ready to aim and fire, when I tripped over a paint can. I felt myself falling backward in slow motion. The monster leaned forward, its gaping mouth opening wide.

I spied Charlie over the monster's shoulder, steadfastly launching another Net. Rather than put my arms down to break my fall, I let my already placed finger swipe up.

My body smashed onto the floor, but luckily my butt landed first. My eyes involuntarily closed as pain shot through me. I expected to feel the monster's dripping goo on me next, but I reopened my eyes to see . . . nothing.

Charlie yelled, "Woo-hoo!" and jumped up and down. "It worked! It's gone!"

I let out a sigh of relief. We did it! We really did it! I checked the Monster Lab on my phone, and there it was. The TeddyGlob was right next to the Uniguin.

"Two down. Eight to go," Charlie said.

I stood up and brushed myself off. "What happened there? You froze."

Charlie's face flushed. "I know. When the monster was coming at me, I just . . . I'm a wimp. I'm an embarrassment."

Whoa, whoa, whoa. Those were Jason's words coming right out of Charlie's mouth, and I didn't like it one bit. "That's not true at all. It was your first time seeing a monster. You had a little moment there, a blip, but you came through in the end. When it counted."

Charlie nodded but didn't seem convinced.

I knew how to raise his spirits. "I think celebratory ice cream is in order while we figure out where to monster hunt next."

Charlie's eyes lit up. "Ice Cream Shack?"

I raised my hand up for a high five. "Absolutely."

We walked downtown toward Charlie's favorite ice cream place. My stomach was still a little wobbly, but we deserved a reward. The TeddyGlob wasn't a difficult monster in the game, but in real life, that was a close call. How would we manage to catch the scarier monsters?

I pushed the thought away. Ice cream first. Worry later.

We were passing the library when a girl I recognized from my short stint in dance class came rushing out the front door. She kept glancing over her shoulder, like she was a little freaked out.

"Hey, Bex," she said. "Don't bother. They're not letting people in."

I skipped over the part about how I wasn't heading into the library and was actually headed toward ice cream. "Why? What's going on?"

"They're having an electrical problem."

The tiny hairs on my arms stood on end. I spoke slowly. "What kind of electrical problem?"

Chloe shrugged. "Power surges or something. The lights were going crazy. I heard someone scream. And then Mrs. Dorsey kicked us all out."

Charlie and I exchanged a look. Ice cream would have to wait.

6

didn't even think about the library," Charlie said as we walked up the steps. "It's a brand new building."

"Yeah, but it was built on the same site as the old one. That must count."

I jiggled the doorknob, but it was locked. Mrs. Dorsey, one of the librarians, played *Monsters Unleashed*. So she could see them, too. We needed to let her know we could help. And after we caught whatever was currently terrorizing the library, maybe Mrs. Dorsey would help us take them *all* down.

Charlie and I pounded on the door. I peered through the glass. Every light in the building buzzed and flared. If electrical stuff going wonky was a sign of a monster nearby, the library had something big.

Suddenly, a pale face appeared against the glass.

"Holy helium!" Charlie exclaimed. He'd recently memorized the periodic table of elements—for fun— and it popped out of him at interesting times.

The face on the other side of the glass was Ms. Bloom, the reference librarian, who'd probably been working there when Grandpa Tepper's map was created.

"The library's closed!" she yelled through the door.

"Mrs. Dorsey needs our help!" I called back. "Let us in. We know what to do."

She squinted behind a pair of glasses so thick they could have been used as a telescope. Then, apparently satisfied with what she saw, she unlocked the door.

Charlie and I quickly pushed our way in and locked the door behind us.

"Where is it?" Charlie asked.

"Where's what?" Ms. Bloom said, confused. "You here to help with the technology, right? You young people know all about the gadgets."

I gave Charlie a little elbow in the side that said *play along.*

"Yes, of course," he said. "The power surges are probably caused by the waffle-mater in the intra-netweb. We're going to check it out."

She nodded. "I'll stay here and keep telling people we're closed until it's back under control."

"Good plan," I said.

Mrs. Dorsey was smart to send Ms. Bloom to the door, where she wouldn't get hurt. Charlie and I, on the other hand, ran right toward the trouble.

"Ugh." Charlie rubbed his nose. "This smells worse than Jason's sneakers."

The library usually smelled like books, which was the second-best smell in the world after pizza. But right now it was pretty rank in here. These monsters needed to discover the wonders of deodorant.

The front desk was empty, as was the line of computers visitors were allowed to use. A loud bang and a shriek came from the Teen Room. I knew that area of the library well. I'd borrowed more books than I could remember. We worked our way toward the sound, keeping close to the wall.

Mrs. Dorsey was my favorite librarian. She always

remembered everyone and knew what kind of books they liked. She'd given me awesome recommendations so many times. She had black curly hair, and every day she wore cool dangly earrings. She usually had a smile for everyone.

But today she wasn't smiling.

We found her hiding behind a bookcase, armed with a fire extinguisher. At the sound of our footsteps, she turned, swinging it wildly.

"Whoa!" Charlie yelled, putting his hands up.

"Oh, children." She put her hand over her chest. "You shouldn't be in here."

"Which monster is it?" I asked, getting right to the point.

Her eyes widened. "You've seen it, too?"

"There are a lot of them in town today. Real ones. What's in here?"

Her lower lip trembled in fear. "A FurClaw."

I took a deep breath. Okay, that was moderately scary. FurClaws were huge, with violent strength. But it was three against one, and I liked those odds.

I gazed down at the fire extinguisher in her hands. "That won't do any damage. You need to use the game."

She dropped the extinguisher and pulled her

phone out of the pocket of her dress pants. "For real? It works?"

"It's a long story," I began to explain. "But all the monsters are mine. They escaped from my Lab into the real world. We've already put two back in. We just need to catch the rest of them. You do it just like in the game."

She peered over her shoulder. "I don't know if I can."

"We're here with you. The three of us, together?" I looked at Charlie and smiled. "We got this."

Mrs. Dorsey straightened and pointed farther into the library. "It was heading toward Sci-Fi."

"Fitting," Charlie deadpanned.

We inched along the wall, peering through bookshelves, aisle by aisle, until finally, we saw it. The FurClaw had a giant puppy-dog face with floppy ears, which didn't sound scary, but the rest of its body was that of a lion. It opened its mouth and roared through its fangs, the sound so loud it made the floor shake. It swiped a huge paw across the top of a shelf, knocking all the books over, except one that clung to its six-inch claws. It shook its paw, and the book released. I ducked my head as the thick hardcover went sailing over me.

"It looks angrier than my brother on report card day," Charlie muttered.

"On the count of three," I whispered. "One."

We all held our phones up.

"Two."

The apps were open. Our battle weapons ready.

I inhaled deeply. "Three!"

Mrs. Dorsey and I sprung out from behind the shelving, but Charlie stayed behind, seemingly rooted to the ground. His eyes were wide and his body trembled slightly. Mrs. Dorsey started launching Battle-Nets at the FurClaw. I tried to fling a few of my own, but I was distracted by Charlie's behavior.

"C'mon, dude!" I yelled. "Get up here!"

"I'll . . . I'll just mess it up," he stammered. "I'm not good at this."

"Yes, you are! We need you! Come on!"

He blinked a few times and his body moved forward robotically, like he was forcing every step.

"Simultaneously now!" I cried. Mrs. Dorsey, Charlie, and I held our phones out high, like the three musketeers of nerds, and launched BattleNets at the same time. The monster roared and swiped at them with his giant claw-paws. We launched again and again, weakening him.

Mrs. Dorsey let out an excited whoop as the Fur-Claw took a defeated step back. She was awesome at this. We were going to take this monster down, and then she'd help us get all the others, too. Even the terrifying nighttime ones. We could have this whole problem done and over with by morning! Confidence welled inside of me.

"What is all that racket?" Ms. Bloom came strolling in, a frown the size of Texas on her face.

The FurClaw roared again, rattling the room. Two books fell from their shelves to the floor. But to Ms. Bloom, who couldn't see the monster, the whole thing looked suspicious.

"Who's doing that?" she snapped. "This isn't funny. One of you is going to pick those up."

Ignoring her, Charlie and I launched another BattleNet simultaneously, but the FurClaw jumped to the left, dodging our throws.

At the sight of Charlie and me "playing" on our phones rather than fixing whatever we were supposed to be fixing, Ms. Bloom's face turned bright red.

She pointed a finger at us. "Hey! No cell phone use in the library."

"Not now, Bianca!" Mrs. Dorsey yelled, launching a BattleNet of her own.

Ms. Bloom charged over, ready to give us all a piece of her mind.

"Stop right there!" Mrs. Dorsey yelled.

Shocked, Ms. Bloom froze. She didn't know it, but the FurClaw was standing right next to her, sniffing at her white hair.

Mrs. Dorsey put her hands up. "Don't. Move."

"Why in heavens not?" Ms. Bloom asked and went to cross her arms.

The sudden movement startled the FurClaw, who lashed out at her and then ran away. I thought I spied it bounding toward the Biography section, but before we could follow, we had to tend to Ms. Bloom. A line of red had appeared down her arm beneath her white blouse.

She winced in pain. "What was that?"

Charlie and I looked at each other. "It was a . . . um . . . cat."

"A cat?" she repeated. "I didn't see a cat."

"It was a ninja cat," Charlie said quickly.

"A stray cat," I corrected. "It was really fast."

"That's probably what's been messing with the electrical system," Mrs. Dorsey said. "The cat must have chewed through a wire somewhere."

Ms. Bloom squeezed her arm, frowning. "I'm going to get this checked out at my doctor. I could have rabies. But these books better be cleaned up when I get back!"

"They will be," Mrs. Dorsey said, sounding relieved. "Please lock the door behind you."

With a huff, Ms. Bloom grabbed her purse from her desk and left the building. Now we were alone with the monster. And it was stuck in here with us. Three against one. It was going down.

"Oh, no!" Charlie cried.

My head snapped toward him. "What?"

"The app shut down!"

"What?" I looked down at my phone. "Mine's working fine."

"My mom must have put a time limit on it somehow," he said. "When she said only an hour, she really meant it."

And then there were two of us. Wonderful. It was a good thing we hadn't eaten lunch yet because I might have thrown it up right then.

Mrs. Dorsey clapped a hand on my shoulder. "It's okay. We girls got this."

I looked up, and she gave me that familiar smile. She was right. Charlie and I had taken down a Teddy-Glob together—only the two of us. Sure, a FurClaw was more of a challenge, but we could do this.

"I have a plan," Charlie said.

The three of us huddled together and whispered until we reached an agreement. It was a risky move, but it made sense. The FurClaw was too good at knocking the BattleNets away. We had to catch it by surprise.

Mrs. Dorsey and I took the long way down the History aisle while Charlie went right, where Biography met Audiobooks. I knew we were getting closer to the FurClaw because I could hear its angry growls. And it smelled like wet dog.

Charlie's plan was to keep the monster distracted and facing one direction so that Mrs. Dorsey and I could battle him from the back. Before the FurClaw knew what was happening, it'd be defeated and back in my Lab.

Mrs. Dorsey and I each held our breath and listened from the aisle behind the monster as Charlie crept down the aisle in front of it. As planned, Charlie pushed a book, causing it to fall from the shelf onto the floor in front of the FurClaw.

Looking confused and angry, the FurClaw picked up the offending book and launched it all the way to the children's room.

Then Charlie did it again.

And again. And again.

He dashed down the aisle, pushing books so that they'd fall to the monster's clawed feet. And it worked. He had the FurClaw's undivided attention. And anger. Its huffing and puffing intensified into a roar, even louder than before. So loud that the ground beneath our feet shuddered and shook.

As the FurClaw raged at the opposite shelf, Mrs. Dorsey quietly removed three books in front of us, leaving just enough space for us to aim our phones at the monster's back and do battle. But before we even launched our first Net, the plan went terribly wrong.

In a flash of anger, the FurClaw threw its weight against the bookcase that kept mysteriously throwing books at it. The entire section of shelving came crashing down. Where Charlie had been standing.

An involuntary gasp burst out of me, and the FurClaw whipped around and turned its dark eyes on us.

"Stay here and keep battling," Mrs. Dorsey ordered. "No matter what!"

I needed to get to that bookcase. I needed to make sure Charlie wasn't underneath it. I needed to know that he was okay.

But Mrs. Dorsey was right. No one would be okay if we didn't capture this monster. I had to do this first.

I launched a BattleNet as the FurClaw raged toward me, claws raised in the air. But then a voice redirected his attention.

"Hey, you big stinker!" called Mrs. Dorsey. "Come and get me!"

She waved her arms above her head, teasing the monster. It took the bait, charging after her. And from the shock and fear on her face, I think that's where her brilliant plan ended. So she did what anyone would do. She ran.

I followed close behind, launching BattleNet after BattleNet at the monster's back while its attention was focused on trying to catch and eat my favorite librarian. It was hard to run and launch at the same time. My finger kept slipping across the screen as the phone bounced up and down. But I kept at it, reminding myself that I was great at this game. This was my thing. I could do this.

Except I wasn't launching fast enough. Mrs. Dorsey didn't have much more room to run. The FurClaw closed in, so close that its last swipe almost reached Mrs. Dorsey's flowing blouse. She dodged it, taking a quick right to hide down the Mystery books aisle. I had a moment to stop moving and then I made the perfect throw. Sometimes you just feel it. This was the one.

The FurClaw felt the BattleNet hit it, square in the back. It lashed out with both arms, pushing at nearby shelving. Then it was zapped into the air, quick and bright like a lightning strike.

"You did it!" A voice screeched from behind me.

Charlie ran over with a bit of a limp, and I threw my arms around his neck. "You're okay!"

"Yeah," he said. "I had to climb out from under a pile of nonfiction. But I'm fine. Where's Mrs. Dorsey?"

My heart stopped and restarted.

The shelving. As I hit the FurClaw with my direct shot, it pushed over one last bookcase. And it had fallen very close to where Mrs. Dorsey had gone to hide.

I inched over to the damaged section and gingerly looked down. Mrs. Dorsey was crumpled on the ground, hands gripping a leg that was totally pointed the wrong way.

"The shelf fell on it." She gasped in obvious pain. "I think it's broken."

Charlie grimaced, looking a little sick at the sight. "I'm no doctor but, yeah, it definitely is."

I was so grossed out, I could barely speak. I managed to squeeze out, "You'll be okay" as I made eye contact with anything in the room except her leg that pointed west while her body pointed east.

We waited with Mrs. Dorsey until the ambulance came, and as the EMTs strapped her to the stretcher, she motioned for me to lean in.

She whispered in my ear. "Promise me you'll catch the rest. More people are going to get hurt . . . or worse. You have to save the town."

I clasped her hand in mine and squeezed. "I will. I'll get them all. I promise."

Her eyes got glassy. "I wish I could help."

"I wish you could, too. But you have to get fixed up. Plus, I always have Charlie."

Her face lit up. "Maybe there is something! My phone is on the ground where I got knocked down. Give it to Charlie. Then he won't have to worry about any time limits."

"Won't you need it?" I asked.

"I'll have a regular phone in my hospital room. Bring my cell back to me after you've caught all the monsters."

"I will," I promised.

The library was a disaster area, but when Ms. Bloom found out she didn't have rabies, she'd get a crew to come in here and fix that mess the naughty stray cat made.

In the meantime, I wanted to see the fruit of our labor. I opened the Monster Lab on my phone and readied myself to see the FurClaw back where it belonged.

Instead, I gasped.

Charlie rushed to my side. "What?"

I looked up at him. "You're not going to believe this."

stared down at the phone in my hand, not immediately understanding what I was seeing. The Uniguin, TeddyGlob, and FurClaw were all back in my Monster Lab as expected. But so were my other Uniguin and my Zebot. And I hadn't caught those.

Charlie took the phone from my hand, and a confused expression slipped over his face. "But we didn't catch the Zebot. Or the second Uniguin. How did they get back in?"

A realization came over me. "If we didn't catch them, someone else did. We've got some help." I paused, thinking. "But the question is . . . who?"

Charlie handed the phone back. "Is there any way to find out who's doing it?"

I shook my head. "Not unless we spot them mid battle."

Charlie frowned. "It figures they got the two easy ones. Couldn't they have gotten the VampWolf or the SpiderFang?"

"That's why I really wish we knew who it was. We could work together. We need the help."

Charlie's stomach made a sound similar to that of a mini-FurClaw. "First, we need food. I can't keep battling on an empty stomach."

Since we were already downtown, we decided to stop at Bodhi's Diner, which served lunch but, more importantly, breakfast all day. And they had the best pancakes in town. It was owned by the family of our classmate Vanya Patel, and she was often hanging out inside helping her parents. So I wasn't surprised to see her when we walked in the door.

"Hey, guys!" she said brightly. Her long black hair

swung as she walked toward us. Then she stopped, and her mouth dropped open. "Why do you look like you've had the longest day of your life and it's only like one o'clock?"

I looked at Charlie and he looked at me. He had a smudge of dirt on his cheek. His T-shirt was covered in dust, probably from being buried under a bookcase. And his hair forked out in a thousand different directions. From the bemused look on his face, my appearance probably wasn't much better.

I turned back to Vanya. "Oh, we've been defending the town from monsters all day."

She let out a belly laugh. "You two! Still obsessed with that game, huh?"

"You know us," I said with an awkward chuckle. I wished I could tell her the truth, but she wouldn't believe me. She'd never played the game.

Vanya led us toward a booth by the front window and plopped down two menus, though we wouldn't really need them. We always got the same things—blueberry pancakes for me and chocolate chip for Charlie. After we put in our order and the waitress brought us sodas, we leaned back in the booth and sighed.

Charlie chuckled. "And to think a couple days ago, all I was worried about was middle school."

I blinked quickly. Charlie, too? I thought I was the only one who sat around thinking about the worst-case scenarios our new school could bring.

I leaned forward, putting my elbows on the table. "You're worried about school? Like what?"

He played with his straw, stirring the ice around in his drink. "Well, it sounds terrible. There's no recess."

I laughed. "Anything more . . . important?"

He stopped stirring and looked at me. "What if we're not in any classes together? And we don't share the same lunch period? Without recess . . ."

"We'd never see each other anymore?"

He gazed down at the table. "Yeah."

"Not going to happen," I said. "We're neighbors, remember? Even if we don't see each other in school, we'll walk home together every day. And you can do your homework at my house. Just like last year."

"Promise?" He held out his pinky.

I wrapped my pinky around his and shook. "We'll always be friends." I paused for a moment. "Unless one of us gets eaten by a monster."

"I wish that wasn't an actual possibility right now. How crazy is this situation?"

"Mega crazy. Peak crazy. Your brother on Meatless Mondays crazy."

Charlie snorted soda out of his nose. "He does hate my mom's famous zucchini noodle casserole." He smiled guiltily. "It's become my favorite day of the week."

We both snickered and laughed until the pancakes came, and then it was like *we* were the monsters. We tore into those pancakes like savage beasts, not speaking until our plates were empty and our stomachs distended.

"I'm too full to monster hunt," I moaned.

"I don't think I can stand up," Charlie said back.

"We should take a few minutes to strategize. Figure out what we're doing next."

Charlie pulled out Mrs. Dorsey's phone with its gold, glittery case. "What daytime monsters are left?"

I looked up at the ceiling as I counted off on my fingers. "The SharkFace, OinkCat, and FireWing." Considering how much of a disaster catching the FurClaw was, I really wasn't looking forward to the rest. All three of those would be more difficult. Mrs. Dorsey already had a broken leg. We could get really hurt, or worse.

"You know what we need?" Charlie said. "Hypnosis Tonic."

It wasn't a bad idea. When used against a monster, Hypnosis Tonic made it dizzy and weak for a few moments, giving you a quick tactical advantage. Unfortunately, unlike the app itself, Hypnosis Tonic was an add-on and had to be purchased with real money. And I'd just spent all of mine on pancakes.

"Do you have any money left?" I asked. "Because mine just went to my stomach."

He turned his pocket inside out and dumped everything he had on the table. It added up to two dollars and thirteen cents.

"How much is the Tonic?" he asked.

We'd never used it before. My mom was already upset with me for playing *Monsters Unleashed* all the time. If I started asking for money to play the game, it would really cause an issue. I opened up the app and checked the price.

I groaned. "Ten bucks."

Charlie sank back in his seat. "My mom will never give me that. In fact, she's probably writing up a punishment list right now because I've had her phone too long."

My mom wouldn't hand over the money either. But it was possible she'd let me earn it.

I slapped my hands together. "Okay, we should probably get home. You have to return your mom's phone. And keep Mrs. Dorsey's phone hidden!"

"But what about the Tonic?"

"I'll work on getting the money for that. You have your own job to do."

"What's that?" he asked warily.

"Ask your grandpa to whip up a batch of his famous sauce. Extra garlic." I straightened in my seat. "Tonight . . . we get the VampWolf."

8

reached my hand down, grasping my enemy by its root. Then I twisted, turned, and pulled until I felt it release from the flower bed. The weed lay in my hand, defeated. I stuffed it into the garbage bag with the rest of its kind, then stood and wiped the dirt off my knees. I surveyed the land before me. Only a few weeds left and I'd be done.

Sweat trickled down my back. I reached for the glass of water on the patio table and chugged until it was gone. I couldn't believe the town was being overrun by monsters, I was one of the few people who could save it, and I was weeding a garden. But it was a necessary part of the plan.

The back door squeaked and opened, and my mom came outside carrying a fresh glass of water.

"Thanks," I said, and gulped greedily.

She inspected the flower beds. "They look wonderful, Bexley. You're doing a great job." Then she turned to me and smiled. It was that "proud mom" smile that I got every once in a while that usually prefaced one of her mom-speeches.

"I just want to tell you," she began.

And here it comes.

"I'm really proud of the way you went about this. You know I don't approve of wasting dollars on those mobile games. But instead of coming up to me begging for money, you asked to earn it. And you worked hard. That's why I just put ten dollars in your account. Responsibility and a good work ethic will get you everywhere."

"Thanks, Mom." I felt my cheeks redden. I liked the proud-mom speeches. They were much better than the disappointed-mom speeches. But they did make me feel a little embarrassed.

A strand of hair that had escaped my ponytail tickled my cheek. Mom tucked it behind my ear and gave my shoulder a pat. "Okay, then. You have a few more weeds by the rosebushes and then you and Charlie can go off and have fun."

Yep, have fun. That is totally what we're going to do.

"We're having dinner at Grandpa Tepper's house," I said.

"Oh, I think that's wonderful that you two keep him company from time to time."

Yeah, and we don't get into any trouble over there at all.

Grandpa Tepper burped like a TeddyGlob and wiped his mouth. "Excuse me."

I giggled behind my hand. Charlie sometimes complained that his grandfather was cranky, but he cracked me up. He had a lot of funny stories from "back in the day" that made me laugh. My grandparents lived in Florida, and I only got to see them once a year. But I saw Grandpa Tepper all the time. So much that I'd begun to think of him as my own grandfather. Especially when he did sweet things, like on my last birthday when he gave me a cute purple birdhouse he'd made.

"That was yummy!" I said, pushing my empty plate to the side.

Charlie patted his belly. "Yeah, thanks, Grandpa. I'm stuffed."

Even though we were here under false pretenses, dinner had been as great as always. And I didn't even mind that his sauce had too much garlic. Though there would be a VampWolf tonight who *really* would mind.

Grandpa Tepper eased back in his chair and stared at us, like he was waiting for something. "So . . ."

Charlie and I looked at each other. "So, what?" Charlie asked.

He drummed his fingers on the table. "We've done a lot of chit-chatting about school and what projects I'm working on. But when are we going to get to why you're *really* here?"

I had to stop my jaw from dropping open. Did he know? About the monsters, the VampWolf, why we needed his sauce . . .

Charlie nervously babbled. "Um, I don't know what you're, um, talking, um, about."

Grandpa Tepper groaned, clearly exasperated. "I'm talking about my machine! You two were playing up in the attic and you broke it!"

"Oh, *that*," Charlie said, with obvious relief.

I kicked him under the table. "What Charlie meant to say was, yes, we did come over tonight to tell you we broke your machine. And we're sorry."

He frowned. "Didn't I tell you to be careful up there?"

"You did," Charlie said. "And please don't be mad at Bex. It was my fault. I was the one who pressed the buttons and fried it."

Grandpa Tepper stood, his back cracking like a pile of dry twigs. "I'm not mad at either one of you. Accidents happen. I'm just disappointed that you didn't tell me."

Guilt rose up in me. There was a lot we weren't telling a lot of people right now. But they'd think we were lying and then we'd be in even more trouble. We had to solve this monster problem on our own. Grandpa Tepper couldn't help us.

Well, his sauce could.

"Where did you get that machine anyway?" I asked casually. Like *no big deal. It didn't do anything weird like transfer video game monsters into the real world. Just curious.*

He wiped his mouth with a napkin. "I bought it at an estate sale last year when one of my neighbors up and moved and sold a bunch of his stuff. I'd thought it was a high-end Heathkit Linear Amplifier that I was buying for a steal. But it turned out someone had done some modifications to it, and it was worthless. I could never get it to do anything."

"Why did the guy move?" Charlie asked.

Grandpa Tepper shrugged. "I thought maybe he'd been fired, but I never found out for sure. He worked for that game company in town."

I shot up in my seat. "Veratrum?"

"Yeah, that's the one. Making games for all you kids, turning you into screen zombies . . ."

He continued for a while, complaining about "kids these days," but I had tuned him out. Veratrum Games was headquartered in an office building here in town. But more importantly, it was the maker of *Monsters Unleashed*. Knowing where the machine came from helped to explain things a little, but it didn't solve the problem. We still had to catch the monsters.

I snatched up my plate. "I'll get started on the dishes."

Charlie stood, balled up the napkins from the table, and tossed them into the trash. I gave him a look that said *Now. Remind him.*

He scuffed his shoe back and forth on the floor. "So, um, Grandpa. Did you make that extra sauce I asked for? To bring home?"

Grandpa Tepper opened the fridge and removed a Tupperware container. "Yes, but how did you go through all of the sauce already?" He handed it to Charlie. "I just gave you a container last night."

I turned away and continued washing the dishes. Charlie was nervous enough when he lied. He didn't need me watching.

"Um, I didn't get to have any of the last batch," Charlie said truthfully.

"Well, why not?" Grandpa snapped.

Because he threw it at a monster, I thought.

"Jason and his friends ate it all," Charlie blurted.

Jason—Monster. Close enough.

Grandpa Tepper frowned. "Well, hide this batch if you have to. You can't let your older brother push you around."

I knew in that moment that he was talking about more than sauce. But now was not the time.

"Hey, we have to get going," I said, drying my hands on a dishtowel. "It's getting dark."

I gave Charlie a meaningful look. The nighttime monsters spawned at seven o'clock and it was already seven fifteen. We had to get this show on the road before the VampWolf decided to make some poor person on Nightshade Road its appetizer.

Grandpa Tepper thanked us for coming, and we thanked him for dinner. Charlie held the container of sauce like it was liquid gold in his hands. With one final wave, the door closed behind us and we were out on the sidewalk.

"You ready?" I asked.

"As I'll ever be," Charlie said nervously.

We backtracked toward home, cutting across the common. The closer we got to Nightshade Road, the more I thought eating dinner right before the big confrontation was a bad idea. Grandpa Tepper's chicken parmesan was doing cartwheels in my anxious belly. And Charlie's face was turning an interesting shade of green.

"Why can't you trust atoms?" his trembling voice asked.

Normally I'd complain about another science

joke, but if it made him less nervous, I'd roll with it. "I don't know. Why can't you trust atoms?"

"They make up everything."

I grinned, but I couldn't even force a laugh. And Charlie couldn't either, which wasn't a good sign. He always laughed the hardest at his own jokes.

As we approached the corner of the road, we stopped to take a breath.

"We got this," I assured Charlie, though I was also trying to convince myself.

The last time we faced off with the VampWolf, we dumped sauce and ran away in terror. But things would be different this time. We were armed with phones, extra-garlicky sauce, Hypnosis Tonic, and a flashlight in case the streetlamps went wonky again. We were prepared for anything.

A bloodcurdling scream rang through the night.

Except that.

Charlie stiffened his shoulders. "Who was that?"

"A VampWolf victim," I suggested. "We'd better hurry up."

We came around the corner, phones out, app loaded. Ready for battle. But the street was empty. A person had definitely screamed, though. A terrified person.

"Where did they go?" I asked.

"Maybe they're hiding," Charlie's shaky voice answered. "I wish we were hiding."

Nightshade Road only had two houses and both were dark, thankfully. Wherever those people were, they were safer there than home right now. The historical marker for the old meeting room was just past the houses. But the road was so wooded, the Vamp-Wolf could be hiding behind any tree in the gloom.

I scrunched up my nose. "It smells like wet dog out here."

"So it could be someone's cute little dog?" Charlie said hopefully.

"More likely a Wolf."

The smell intensified as we walked farther down the road. Since the scream, there had been only eerie silence. The road's lone streetlamp flashed like a strobe light. The closer we got to it, the faster it flickered, until finally it went out completely.

"Just like last time," Charlie whispered.

"Except, now we're prepared."

I slid the flashlight out of my pocket and flicked the switch on. I aimed the narrow beam of light at the road in front of us. Empty. Then I scanned the trees on the right. Only shadows that turned out to be nothing. I slowly moved the beam along the trees on the left, then froze, my hand starting to tremble.

Two red eyes peered out between the trees.

A snarl broke the silence.

Charlie started to mutter, "Oh, no. Oh, no. Oh, no!"

"It's okay," I said. "We're prepared. We've got this. You take the right side of the road; I'll stick to the left." That was part of the plan we'd decided on. If the Wolf had to keep its attention divided between the two of us, we had a better shot at overpowering it with our battle tools. I only hoped Charlie wouldn't freeze up this time.

Charlie moved over to the sidewalk on the right and I stepped up onto the left. The VampWolf lurched out of the shadows and toward us, its paws taking slow steps, the brown fur on its back raised. It snarled again, baring its vampire-like fangs. They looked like yellow, sharpened daggers.

Keeping the flashlight steady in one hand, I aimed my phone with the other. The VampWolf was still too far away to catch with a BattleNet, but I needed to be ready. When they wanted to, VampWolves could move with intense speed.

Just as I thought that, it lunged forward, even faster than I'd expected. I shrieked and nearly lost my footing, wobbling on the edge of the curb. My arms waved in the air while I regained my balance. The VampWolf closed in.

"Get away from her!" Charlie yelled suddenly. He puffed out his chest. "Come get me, you big . . . smelly . . . stinkface!"

His trash talk could use some work, but I appreciated the flash of bravery. And it gave me the distraction I needed to steady myself. Time for some Hypnosis Tonic.

I lodged the flashlight under my armpit so I could hold the phone with one hand and manage the app with the other. I selected the newly purchased Hypnosis Tonic and launched it with a swipe.

A haze went over the monster and it swayed in place, making gurgling noises. We had only a few moments. We had to take advantage of it.

"Now!" I said forcefully. "Throw the sauce!"

Charlie tore the lid off the Tupperware and tossed the garlicky concoction right at the VampWolf. The sauce rained down its furry face like acid. Yummy, yummy acid. The VampWolf let out a tortured howl.

"Give it everything you've got!" I ordered.

Charlie and I launched simultaneous BattleNets as the VampWolf started to come out of its hypnotic stupor. It gargled and snarled, bobbed and ducked. But we didn't give up. We launched again and again. And finally, with a roar and a zap of light, the Vamp-Wolf disappeared.

I swiped left and opened up my Monster Lab. A smile so big it almost hurt took over my face. I threw my arms up in victory.

"We did it!" Charlie screeched.

And then, with a rustle and a crash, I realized we weren't alone.

Willa jumped out from behind a trash can, a crazed look on her normally composed face. "Is it gone?"

"Yeah," Charlie said, still beaming proudly from our win.

But I was confused. "It was you? The scream from before?"

She didn't bother to answer. She just jogged away without a word.

Charlie crossed his arms. "So rude. She could've at least thanked us for saving her life."

Willa being rude to me was nothing new. What *was* new, though, was her seeing monsters.

My head whipped toward Charlie. "Willa said, 'Is it gone?' Do you know what that means? She could *see* it."

9

couldn't believe it. Willa Tanaka. The Willa who'd called me all sorts of variations of nerd/dork/geek for playing *Monsters Unleashed* had also played *Monsters Unleashed* herself.

"This explains why she was acting shady that day we saw her at the statue in the common," Charlie said. "She was probably playing the game."

That made sense. But I didn't want to talk about Willa anymore. We'd saved her life and she couldn't even be bothered to say thanks before she took off.

We needed a game plan for catching the remaining monsters.

I opened the photographs of Grandpa Tepper's map on my phone. "Where should we start in the morning?"

Charlie peered over my shoulder. "I say we get up early and head downtown. That's where most of the historical buildings are."

The idea of another day of monster hunting after the long day we'd just had made me feel tired in my bones. How much longer could I do this?

Bright headlights turned the corner as a car came down the road. It pulled into the driveway of one of the houses. A family of four piled out of the car, holding take-out pizza boxes.

"Good timing," I said with a smile.

That family had no idea of the threat that had been lurking in the trees beside their home. They waved at Charlie and me, and we waved back. They probably thought we were simply kids walking around, playing that popular game. They had no idea what we'd just done to keep them safe. And they never would.

I turned back to Charlie. "Yeah, that sounds like a good plan. Let's head home. We've got a big day tomorrow."

I woke early the next morning and walked William Shakespaw without incident. Mrs. Sweeney would be coming back this afternoon, and then I'd be off doggy duty. And I'd even get paid, which would be helpful. We definitely needed to buy more Hypnosis Tonic.

By the time I got back to my house, Charlie was pacing across the driveway.

Confused, I checked the time on my phone. "I'm not late."

"I know," he said, stuffing his hands in the pockets of his shorts. "Let's get going."

He moved so briskly down the sidewalk that I had to almost jog to keep up. I recognized this behavior. It always had one cause—Jason.

"Was your brother being a big farthead this morning?" I asked, hoping for a laugh. Maybe just a giggle. I mean, I had said the word *fart*. That was usually a sure thing.

But Charlie didn't even smile. "I had to get out of there. Jason's up early, getting ready for a big day with his friends. I'd had my fill of insults by the time I'd poured my cereal."

"Sorry," I said, and I meant it. But Charlie really needed to do something about his brother's bullying. He couldn't hide from him all the time. "Maybe you can talk to your parents about Jason."

Charlie rolled his eyes. "I've tried that. They said it's part of having a big brother."

"But they don't know how bad it is. Maybe you could—"

He interrupted. "Listen. It's not going to change. I just have to deal with it. Like you have to deal with Willa."

"That's different," I said. "Jason is your family. He's supposed to, like, love you and stuff."

"Hey, I have a theory," Charlie said, in an obvious ploy to change the subject. "What if Willa is the one helping us catch the monsters?"

I shook my head. "No way."

The Willa I used to know, sure. That Willa was a nerd like me. She loved to play geeky games. And she would have been first in line to save the town from snarling beasts. But the Willa I knew now? Nope. She was a totally different person. Sure, she'd been secretly playing *Monsters Unleashed*. She apparently still had nerdy tendencies somewhere deep inside that she hid from her new, popular friends. But she would never help anyone. Most certainly not me.

Sounds of distress coming down the sidewalk toward us caught my attention. A little boy clung to his mother while he sobbed. I'm talking snot-bubble, hysterical sobbing.

"Is he okay?" I asked as we got closer.

The mom stopped and put the boy down. He looked like he was about four or five, too old to be carried, but the poor kid was terrified.

The woman patted his head and said, "Oh, he thought he saw a monster in the common. But I showed him there was nothing there." Her voice dropped to a whisper. "Overactive imagination on this one."

Charlie and I shared a look.

"Does he play that game, *Monsters Unleashed*?" Charlie asked.

"Yes!" the mom said. "He does. That could be the

cause of this." She looked down and wiped tears off her son's face. "I said you were too young for those games. Mommy was right."

I bent down to get on the same eye level as the little boy. "What kind of monster did you see, buddy?"

"An OinkCat," he whispered, as if saying it too loudly would cause it to spawn right there.

"How about if I promise to catch it? Would that make you feel better?"

The boy nodded and plugged his thumb into his mouth.

"Thanks, kids," the mom said. "Enjoy the nice weather this morning. It's going to be another hot one."

The mother and son scurried off back to their house, and we hurried forward to the common. Hopefully, no one else would be out and about this early. I wanted to get in, catch the OinkCat, and move on.

"Okay," Charlie said as we walked. "Let's game-plan."

I waved my hand. "No need. We caught a Vamp-Wolf last night. We got this." After last night's victory, I was walking with a little swagger in my step.

"Remember the OinkCat's stats," Charlie said.

"It looks unimpressive, but its strength is off the charts."

We rounded the corner and came into full view of the Wolcott Common. That woman had been right. It was a beautiful morning—not too hot, not a cloud in the blue sky, not one piece of trash on the wide expanse of grass.

But somewhere a monster was hiding.

Two young kids and their dad wandered toward us, their eyes scanning the ground.

"Have you seen our ball?" the little girl asked.

"No," Charlie said. "What color is it?"

"Red," the father answered. "It's the strangest thing. We were playing catch. I tossed it in the air and then . . ." His voice drifted off and his cheeks reddened, like he was too embarrassed to finish the sentence.

The girl didn't mind. "The ball stopped in midair, like someone invisible had caught it. And then the ball was just gone. Someone invisible took it!"

The father laughed nervously. "It was a trick of light. It probably rolled somewhere."

"Hey," Charlie said. "Do you guys play that game, *Monsters Unleashed*?"

The dad frowned in kind of a judgy way. "No. I try to limit their screen time."

The kids both rolled their eyes behind him. But it explained why they thought someone invisible had caught their ball. They couldn't see the OinkCat. But he was somewhere out there . . . apparently with a new toy.

"We have to get going, guys," the dad said, hustling his kids away.

"Keep an eye out for our ball!" the girl called over her shoulder.

I breathed a sigh of relief as they left. With an OinkCat on the loose, an empty park was a safe park. Even if all it had done so far was steal some family's ball.

I clapped my hands together. "Okay, let's find this thing." It couldn't be too hard. Most of the common was wide open. The only places the monster could be hiding were behind some trees, the statue, or the gazebo. If we could sneak up on it together, we'd have a tactical advantage.

"Come on out, OinkCat!" Charlie yelled.

And there goes that.

From a distance came a squeal in response. It

could only be described as coming from a half-cat, half-pig, who was 100 percent not happy.

"Let's split up," I said. "I'll look around the statue; you take the gazebo."

Charlie chewed on his bottom lip. "Are you sure that's a good idea?"

"We're not dealing with a SpiderFang here. The first one to find it yells for the other, we team up, and—*Boom! Zap!*—back in the Monster Lab."

Charlie gave me a wary look but trudged off toward the gazebo.

I marched toward the statue. As I passed a thicket of trees, I felt the distinct feeling of eyes on me. I stopped and stared but saw no movement. There wasn't anything electrical in the common that could go haywire, and I didn't smell anything horrid. But that didn't mean a monster wasn't hiding in those trees. I took a step closer. The little hairs on my arms stood on end. Something was definitely in there, hiding and watching me. I knew it in my gut.

"It's here! I found the ball!" Charlie called.

He bent down and picked up a bright red ball at the entrance to the gazebo. Huh. My gut had been wrong. The OinkCat was over there. I started to sprint toward the gazebo just as the OinkCat made its appearance.

The monster was a pig with a cat's face. It had long eyelashes and a little pink nose. In the game, the OinkCat was a feared beast. But in real life, it looked strangely . . . sweet.

It inched toward Charlie, face down, an almost bashful look in its eyes.

"Launch a Net, Charlie!" I said, whipping my own phone out and getting ready.

The monster whimpered, its bottom lip trembling.

Charlie hesitated. "But wait . . . it doesn't seem like the others."

"It's a trick! It's using cuteness as a defense."

But he was falling for it. Probably thinking of all those times he was sad and scared when his brother acted like a jerk. Charlie moved closer, head tilted to the side. "Hey, don't cry. We're not going to hurt you. We just need to put you back where you came from."

He was too close to it. If I launched a Net now, it could strike him with its claws as it tried to dodge. And it would work better if we launched simultaneously.

"Don't fall for it!" I yelled. "Move away!"

"Do you want your ball back? Is that what you want?" He reached his hand out, the red ball in his palm.

The monster's hoof-paw-claw-thing lashed out and knocked the ball out of Charlie's hand. Then, in a feat of surprising strength, it flung Charlie through the air like he was a stuffed animal. He slumped to the ground several feet away, completely knocked out.

Then the monster turned toward me.

I clutched the phone in my sweaty hand. I wished I had more Hypnosis Tonic. I wished I had Charlie battling by my side. But I would have to get this done myself. *You can do this*, I told myself silently. We'd conquered a VampWolf the night before. I wasn't going to let a half pig, half cat take me down.

And the next second, I was down.

The OinkCat had leapt into the air, crossing the distance between us in a second, and knocked me down on the ground.

I reached for my phone, my only defense. *My phone! Where's my phone?* My eyes searched the ground. I spied it on the grass only a few feet away. I rolled onto my stomach and reached for it.

Long claws curled around my ankle. I tried to pull my leg away, but the OinkCat was amazingly strong. It yanked, dragging my body farther away from the phone that I desperately needed. I looked over at Charlie for help, but he was still slumped on the ground, not moving.

Neither of us had our phones. I wasn't strong enough to fight the OinkCat. We were defenseless. R.I.P. Bex and Charlie. This was it. Good-bye, forever.

The OinkCat let go of my ankle and pounced on top of me. That face that I'd found cute only moments before sneered and bared its sharp little teeth. It held one hoof/paw/claw up in the air above me, ready to slash down my body.

And then *POOF!* In a flash of light, the OinkCat *zapped* into the air and disappeared.

"Charlie?" I said, sitting up in shock.

"Nope, definitely not Charlie Tepp-nerd."

10

She stood there with a satisfied smirk on her face.

Willa. Tanaka. Saved. My. Life.

I was speechless.

"Whoa," Charlie said, still sprawled out on the ground but apparently regaining consciousness. "I guess I shouldn't have fallen for the crying act."

Willa carefully brushed some dirt off her cute denim skirt. "I never back down. Even if someone cries."

And for once, I was glad for that.

I rushed to Charlie's side as he tried to sit up. "Are you okay?"

He rubbed the back of his skull. "My head is still attached, right?"

"Um, yeah."

"Then I'm good."

My gut had been right. Someone had been hiding in the trees. Only it wasn't the OinkCat. It was Willa.

I helped Charlie to his feet. He still had Mrs. Dorsey's phone in his hand. I picked a few blades of grass out of his hair and felt the back of his head for a bump. We'd have to stop at his house first before we kept going to make sure he didn't have a concussion. This was one of those times when it was useful that Mrs. Tepper was a nurse.

Willa narrowed her eyes at the phone in Charlie's hand, covered in gold sparkles. "Why does your phone case look like a recycled prom dress?"

He sighed. "It's Mrs. Dorsey's. She gave it—"

Willa put her hand up in front of his face. "I don't even want to know."

I found my phone in the grass and picked it back up.

Willa watched me with her eyes narrowed. "So what did you do?"

I blinked quickly. "Excuse me?"

"The monsters terrorizing the town? I'm assuming this is your fault."

My mouth opened and closed like a fish out of water. I was too frustrated to make words.

"It's no one's fault," Charlie said. "My grandfather had this machine in his attic. I flipped a switch and it somehow zapped Bex's monsters into the real world."

"Oh, so both of you are to blame."

My fists clenched by my sides.

Willa continued prattling on. "I should have known when that Uniguin came out of nowhere that you two had something to do with it. You're lucky I'm secretly good at this stupid game. I captured that monster and a Zebot all in one day. I would have caught the VampWolf, too, if you guys didn't come stumbling down the road."

That did it. I could talk again. "We saved you! You screamed and hid!" I screeched.

Willa put one hand on her hip. "And who did the saving just now, with that OinkCat?"

Ugh. "You," I admitted. "But—"

"And did you even stop to thank me?"

My fists clenched and unclenched again. This girl was getting on my last nerve.

Charlie stepped in between us. "Um, you guys? There are still three monsters out there that need to be caught. Maybe we should do less arguing and more working together."

Willa raised her eyebrows. "Working together?"

He was right. As much as I disliked Willa, working with her was a good idea. The three monsters left were the most difficult to catch and battles were always more successful if you had more players. I had to swallow my pride. And the puke that just came up my throat at the idea of spending time with my ex-friend.

"Charlie is right," I said. "We have a better chance of catching them and keeping everyone in town safe if we work together."

"What monsters are left?" Willa asked.

"A FireWing, a SharkFace, and . . . a SpiderFang."

Willa's eyes widened. "Wow. You *will* need my help." She sighed dramatically and extended her fingers to examine her manicure. "I guess I can make some time."

She had a funky design on her fingernails. My mind

flashed back to a sleepover when she'd done my nails like that. And then we'd watched a horror movie, ate too much popcorn, stayed up too late talking . . .

I stopped myself. That was then. Before Willa dumped me for the popular crowd. Before she lobbed insults at me to make them laugh, like I was a prop in her stand-up comedy show.

Anger churned in my belly. But I forced it away. We had to work together. This was too important. It wasn't about me. It was about the town and the people in it. People I cared about. And if I had to be insulted by Willa while I got the job done, I'd do it.

"Okay, then," I said. "We'll work together."

Charlie beamed at our brokered peace agreement. "So are we . . . friends?"

"No!" Willa scoffed. "More like teammates. And only until these monsters are caught. Then I'm done with you losers."

I closed my eyes and held back a groan. This was going to be harder than I thought.

After a quick break at Charlie's house where his mom confirmed that he was okay and cleared us to "play outside" again, we huddled around my phone in the gazebo back at the common. Now that I was partners with my mortal enemy, it was time to show her all our goods.

"And here's where we are." I pointed to an area on the map photo showing what was now the common but was then known as the Town Square.

"Where did you guys get this?" Willa asked.

Charlie spoke up excitedly. "The original map was in my grandfather's attic. It shows the town as it was in 1856. Isn't it cool?"

"No, nerdbrain. It's not *cool*." She paused. "But it is useful."

Charlie ignored her insult and used his fingers to zoom around the map. "Where could the Shark-Face be?"

I scratched my chin. "We know they like to spawn near water. I caught it down by the lake."

Willa shook her head. "I checked there yesterday. Nothing."

Charlie pointed at the map. "The community pool is built on the site of an old swimming hole."

Willa looked up at him. "Yeah, I remember our history teacher told us they'd had to fill it in because it was all gross with, like, bacteria and stuff. And then they built an actual pool decades later. That's a historical spot. The SharkFace might be hanging out there."

My face lit up. "And the great news is that the pool has been closed all summer because they're putting in a new liner. So if it's there, at least no one's in danger. We can sneak up and—"

"Um, loser?" Willa interrupted.

Under the assumption that she was talking to me, I said, "Yeah?"

"They finished the liner. The pool's grand reopening is today. Everyone knows that. There's going to be a huge party down there."

Oh, no. I looked at Charlie.

He winced. "It's true. That's where Jason and his friends are going."

Willa stood and flipped her hair over her shoulder. "Get your swimsuits, dorks. We're going to a pool party."

11

Willa, Charlie, and I walked into the pool party like the most mismatched trio ever assembled. The humidity had done a number on my hair and, even with a ponytail elastic, it was big enough to warrant its own zip code. Charlie wore a T-shirt with the periodic table of elements. And Willa wore a teeny bikini that fit her perfectly in every way. Luckily, there was enough going on that people didn't seem to notice us.

A Hawaiian-shirt-wearing dad was cooking what

looked like a gazillion hot dogs on a big grill. A million little kids were huddled together in the adjacent kiddie pool, splashing one another and filling up their swim diapers. And Jason and his friends had totally taken over the big pool to play a game of strangely violent water volleyball, in which the goal seemed to be drowning one another rather than hitting the ball.

"So. Many. Jerkfaces." Charlie muttered under his breath.

"So many cute boys," Willa countered. Then she scowled. "And I'm stuck with you two. We'd better get this job done quickly before anyone sees us together."

"Okay," I said, ignoring her jab and readying my phone. "Battle formation. I'll take the left. Charlie you take the right. Willa, you're in between us."

"Like a nerd sandwich," she complained. "Wonderful."

"Scan the water and the grounds around the pool area," I ordered. "Whoever sees the SharkFace first, call out."

"What should we yell?" Charlie asked.

"Yeah, I need a code word," Willa said. "I'm not yelling 'SharkFace' like some total loser."

I sighed. "Okay, Willa. What would you like the code word to be?"

"I don't know. Just something normal."

Charlie piped up. "How about 'hot dogs are ready'? It's something someone would yell out at a pool party. And it might make people run toward the grill, which would keep them out of harm's way while we battle."

Awesome idea. I reached my hand up and gave him a high five.

"Okay, let's do this," Willa said, taking off on her own.

But before Charlie and I could separate, a booming voice yelled, "Hey!"

I turned around slowly, dread churning in my stomach. Not here. Not now.

Jason stood in the shallow end of the pool, surrounded by his friends, all facing Charlie and me. "What are you doing here?" he sneered.

I tried to head the argument off. "It's a town party, Jason."

"I'm not talking to you, Bex. I'm talking to my little brother. The one who knew I was coming here with my bros today. The one who should've used that big brain of his to figure out that I wouldn't want him hanging around."

"We're doing our own thing," I said. "Believe me, we want nothing to do with you."

He crossed his giant muscled arms. "Oh, really? What are you guys doing? Partying with a bunch of your friends?" He laughed at his own lame joke and then gave his friends a look until they snickered along with him.

"C'mon, Charlie." I tugged on his arm. "We've got stuff to do."

"Hold up," Jason said. He told his "bros" to keep playing death-match volleyball without him, and he climbed out of the pool and came toward us.

All the muscles in my body stiffened. It was an instinctual thing, like when our ancestors saw a lion in the wild.

He came up close to Charlie and me and lowered his voice. "You know I'm only giving you a hard time, right, kid?"

Um, what? Was that his version of an apology? What was happening right now? I looked up in the sky to make sure pigs weren't flying.

"Sure," Charlie said with a shrug.

Jason patted him on the shoulder. "Cool." He made like he was about to walk away, and then stopped. "Oh, yeah. One more thing. Grandpa asked me to help him put an air conditioner in his window today. But I don't really have time with the party and all, so you can do it."

Wow. So that half-hearted apology wasn't really an apology after all. He was just buttering Charlie up before he dropped a chore on him. One that Grandpa Tepper had specifically asked Jason to do. And now Charlie was going to give in and do it, and I'd have to catch the SharkFace alone with Willa.

"No," Charlie said.

Jason froze. "Excuse me?"

"I'm actually really busy. And Grandpa didn't ask me. He asked you. You're bigger and stronger. The job would be easier for you. So, you're doing it."

A smile spread across Jason's face. Not a nice smile. An "I'm going to murder you now" smile. "I'm doing it?" he asked.

Charlie sighed. "Jason, I don't want to fight with you. I don't have the time, actually. See you later."

He started to walk away, but Jason grabbed his arm. Hard. Like hard enough to leave fingerprint marks the next day. "Tell me what you're so busy doing," he said between gritted teeth.

Lie, I thought. *Make something up. Or just run. Do anything other than tell him the truth.*

"I'm catching monsters," Charlie said.

The fact that we weren't telepathic was really inconvenient at times.

Charlie continued, "The monsters from our game got zapped into the real world. We've been capturing them before they do too much damage. But people have already been hurt. Mrs. Dorsey from the library has a broken leg. There are only three monsters left, and I have no time for anything right now except catching them."

"I know you're lying and you just want to spend the day playing more levels or whatever. But I don't care about your stupid game," Jason said, his face contorting with anger. "I'm not leaving this party. You have to do this or Mom and Dad will be mad."

Charlie's eyes took on a look I'd never seen before. It was like something inside of him snapped. He puffed his chest out and stepped right up to Jason's face. Well, his collarbone, actually, because Jason was much taller.

He poked a finger into the center of Jason's chest. "I'm sick of you pushing me around, and I'm not going to stand for it anymore. You do what Grandpa Tepper asked you to do, or I'm going to tell Mom and Dad *everything*. I'm going to tell them what an awful brother you are. That you have friends over when you're not supposed to. That you bully me. And now that you don't even care enough about your own grandfather to help him when he asks!"

Jason's jaw dropped so low, I thought it had become unhinged. I looked back and forth between them, expecting Jason to totally hulk-out any moment now and lift Charlie above his head like a rag doll. His face was as red as a fire truck, and a little muscle in the side of his face twitched and pulsed. Yep, Charlie was dead.

"Hot dogs are ready!" Willa shouted.

Saved by the monster. I grabbed Charlie and pulled him away, "Sorry, Jason! We've got to go!"

I ran toward Willa's screeching voice, which was

getting increasingly louder every time she repeated the line. "I SAID HOT DOGS ARE READY, GUYS! COME ON!"

Charlie pointed at a blue and white shed that the town used to store pool equipment. "She must be behind that."

We took the corner and skidded to a stop behind the shed. Sure enough, there was Willa, facing off against an actual, real-life SharkFace. It had—you guessed it—the face of a shark, but it also had slimy legs and a reptilian tail. So it could walk on land like a crocodile. And it smelled like an open can of tuna in a room full of feet.

I looked around. We were hidden behind the shed. We could get down to business without anyone seeing or getting hurt. As long as we were quick.

"Battle formation!" I yelled.

Willa stayed in the middle while Charlie and I spread out to the sides. This confused the dim-witted SharkFace, who gnashed its teeth in my direction, then Charlie's, but because it couldn't quite decide who to eat first, we were able to move in.

"Now!" I roared.

Charlie squared his shoulders and faced off against the monster like he never had before. The three of us launched simultaneous BattleNets again and again. The SharkFace writhed and ducked. It even tried eating one of the Nets. But it was quickly overwhelmed by our coordinated teamwork. With a *zap* and a flash of light, it left this world and landed back in my app.

We exchanged a round of high-fives. This was the easiest take-down yet. We'd worked great as a team. Standing up to Jason seemed to have given Charlie new confidence.

"Now that was a take-down," Willa said, wiping her forehead. "I hope the last two are that easy."

I did, too. But I had a bad feeling that wasn't going to be the case.

After a quick snack break (the hot dogs from the grill actually *were* ready), we set back out. We had one daytime monster left—the FireWing. But we hit up all the old buildings downtown and found nothing. I was starting to get worried. It was six o'clock. The daytime monsters despawned at seven o'clock, opening the world to nighttime monsters. So we had only one hour left to find it, or we'd have to continue the search in the morning.

The three of us sat on a park bench by the edge of a playground. My feet were throbbing. I was sweaty. Charlie smelled like an old sock. Even Willa had some tired bags under her eyes. Oh, wait, that was just a shadow. I sighed.

"Let's look at the map again," Charlie said. "Maybe there's someplace we missed."

I tapped my phone's screen and opened the photo. We'd searched everywhere. There had to be something we were missing. Maybe somewhere historical that wasn't marked on the map.

My phone trilled a little song.

"Hey, T-Bex," Willa said tiredly. "Your map is ringing."

A gasp caught in my throat. T-Bex was a cute nickname Willa had given me when I went through a phase when I wanted to be a paleontologist. I hadn't heard her say it since we stopped being friends. It was an old habit. But she caught herself and quickly looked away like there was something really interesting over her right shoulder.

I gazed down at my phone. I didn't recognize the number. I usually ignored those calls, but something in my gut told me to pick it up.

I slid the ANSWER button and placed the phone up to my ear. "Hello?"

"Is my stupid brother with you?" Jason asked, by way of greeting.

"Yes," I replied curtly.

"Well, can I talk to him?"

"It depends. Are you going to be nice?"

"I don't have time for nice. I think you guys were telling the truth. About those . . . monsters."

My heart sped up. "Why do you believe us now?"

"Because I'm at my grandpa's house helping him with his air conditioner. And we are definitely not alone."

12

We ran all the way to Grandpa Tepper's house. After the day of walking we'd already had, my muscles were practically screaming, but adrenaline kept me going. We had to protect Grandpa Tepper. And to a lesser extent, Jason. I guess. Since he was there, too. Ugh.

The three of us skidded to a stop in front of his house. It was old, with peeling white paint and a saggy front porch, but not historically old. I didn't understand why the FireWing was drawn to the property.

"We're coming, Grandpa!" Charlie called as he charged up the stairs to the house.

Willa and I followed closely behind. The front door was unlocked. I braced myself for the disaster I would see inside, but everything looked normal. Well, normal for Grandpa Tepper. He wasn't really a fan of throwing things out: The kitchen table had a pile of old newspapers. Dirty dishes climbed up the sides of the sink. Little knickknacks were clustered on every available space.

"This place is a disaster area." Willa crinkled up her nose. "Does a FireWing aggressively throw junk everywhere? Is that what they do?"

"My grandfather is a collector," Charlie said defensively. "And as you already know, a FireWing breathes fire."

FireWings were giant, oversized vultures with the faces of dragons. And, um, dragon fire. Which was the scary part. I shuddered. If the FireWing had been in here, there would be damage. I would at the very least smell that monster stench. But all my nose detected was that Jason had gotten a free, garlicky dinner before things went wrong. There was no sign of any monster.

There was also no sign of Jason or Grandpa Tepper.

"Grandpa!" Charlie called. "Jason?"

"In here," a muffled voice responded.

We followed the sound to the bathroom. Charlie tried to turn the knob, but it was locked.

"Unlock the door," Charlie said.

"Is it out there?" Grandpa Tepper asked in a trembling voice.

We each took a cursory glance over our shoulders and shrugged.

"It doesn't look like it," Charlie said at the closed door. "Where did you see it?"

"We didn't *see* anything," Jason said. "But when we walked out back to get the air conditioner out of the shed, something was out there. And it burned a hole in the shed! Like with actual flames. Whatever it is, it's invisible, but big. It was breaking branches as it charged toward us."

Yep, that was a FireWing, and it seemed to like the woods behind Grandpa Tepper's house.

"You can come out of there," I said. "The FireWing didn't follow you inside or anything."

The door slowly pulled open and two terrified faces peered out.

"The fire what?" Grandpa Tepper asked.

"Let's have a seat," Charlie said.

We all settled onto the worn sofas in the living room. Jason looked more confused than he normally did.

Grandpa Tepper pointed a shaky finger at Willa. "Who's that girl? Is she your girlfriend, Charlie?"

"Um, no," Charlie answered, cheeks reddening.

"Gross." Willa's mouth turned down. "And why does this place smell like an abandoned Italian restaurant?"

"Yes, it's a lovely smell," I piped up. "Grandpa Tepper is a great cook. I always get so hungry when I'm here!"

"Can someone tell me what's going on?" Grandpa Tepper said, losing his patience.

I took a deep breath and told him about the night we went up to his attic. I explained that when we broke his machine, the monsters in my phone got transported into the real world.

He sat back, taking it all in. Then he asked, "Why didn't you two tell me what really happened? Why didn't you tell me what was going on?"

Charlie and I looked at each other. I mean, it was obvious.

"We didn't think you'd believe us," Charlie said. "People can only see the monsters if they've played the game. So we had no evidence to show you."

He snorted. "There's enough evidence now with the smoke coming out of my burned shed."

"What else is back there?" Willa asked. "We can't figure out why the FireWing would be on your property."

Grandpa Tepper scratched at the white stubble on his chin. "The shed backs up to the woods, but there's nothing in those trees except some deer and the old carriage house."

I sat up straight. "The what?"

"Oh, yeah," Jason said. "Charlie and I used to play in there when we were little."

Charlie scoffed, "If by play, you mean you would lock me in there pretending it was a jail."

Jason rolled his eyes. "Cops and robbers. Every kid plays that."

"You left me in there for hours!" Charlie yelled.

"Okay, okay." I put my hands out, trying to calm the vibe in the room. "Is there any historical significance to the carriage house?"

"Well, it's all run down now," Grandpa Tepper

said. "I think the roof caved in a couple winters ago. But, yes, there's some significance. The carriage house and the surrounding woods used to belong to John Wolcott, the town's founder."

I gasped. "Why wasn't that marked on the map?"

"Probably because his main house burned down and he relocated to the downtown area. All that was left of his property was that carriage house."

"Where was his main house?" I asked.

"His property spanned several acres. The main house was about an acre away. There's a marker. Didn't you children pay attention on your field trip to the Historical Society?"

We should have. It would've helped us out this week. I pulled the map of town up on my phone. I placed my finger behind Grandpa Tepper's house, where the FireWing was hanging out. About an acre away would be . . . I slid my finger over. It would be where the edge of the woods met the newest construction in town. Now we knew where both monsters were.

Charlie followed my line of thinking immediately. "The FireWing is here and the SpiderFang is in the woods by the middle school!"

"The spider what?" Grandpa Tepper asked.

"I don't even want to know," Jason said, waving his hands in the air. "Can we do fewer history lessons and more FireWing butt kicking?"

"You're not doing anything," Charlie said. "You're staying here with Grandpa while we take care of it."

Jason let out a loud laugh. "What, you're going to fight a monster, noodle arms? You need me."

"Your muscles won't help you here, Jason," I said. "Let us do our job."

"How are you going to do anything to a monster you can't see?" he fired back. "I'll punch that thing repeatedly until I find its face."

"Because *we* can see it," Charlie said. "The only way to see the monsters is to have played the game a bunch of times. And the only way to fight the monsters is to *use* the game."

I stood up. "Leave this to us, Jason."

He muttered something under his breath about nerds as we started to leave the room.

But Grandpa Tepper held up a finger. "Wait one minute."

He dashed upstairs, and we heard him digging around in the attic. After a little while, he came back down holding a camouflage jacket.

"Unfortunately, I only have one of these from my time in the military," he said. "But it might be of help. It's fire resistant."

Charlie took the jacket from his hand and examined it. "Wow, thanks!" Then he turned toward me and held the jacket out. "You wear it."

"Aww, how sweet," Willa said sarcastically. "Nerd love."

Charlie's face turned bright red, and I just wanted the awkward moment to end, so I grabbed the jacket and slid my arms through. "Thanks. You're right. I should wear it because I'm in the center of our battle formation. Literally, in the line of fire."

"Okay," Charlie said to Jason and Grandpa Tepper. "You two stay put, no matter what. We'll be back in a few minutes."

"Hopefully," Willa mumbled. Always a ray of sunshine, that one.

We went out the back door and took tentative steps into the yard. The shed had stopped smoking, but one side of it was charred from the FireWing's breath. The scent of burnt wood and branches permeated the air. As we passed the shed and crossed into the woods, I knew the monster was near. Mostly because the air suddenly smelled like a combination of morning breath and deviled eggs. A classic monster stench.

At least it wasn't dark yet. The sun was setting, slashes of red across the sky, but the woods still had light. The smell increased. A twig cracked nearby. The monster was coming this way.

"Battle formation," I whispered.

We moved to our spots and readied our phones. A branch broke off a nearby tree and fell to the ground. From behind the tree came what looked like a giant vulture with smooth, black feathers and long, clawed talons.

"Nice birdie-birdie," Charlie whispered. "Who's a good bird? Polly want a cracker?"

After its body came into full view, its head turned toward us. It was a deep, dark red with scales and two horns protruding from the top. Smoke drifted out of its nostrils, and a long line of crooked teeth hung over its closed mouth. An orthodontist's nightmare.

I steeled myself for battle. This was going to be a big one. But before we even made our first move, the FireWing rushed at us. And because we were professionals by this point, we totally kept our composure.

Nah, we didn't. We all screamed and backed up.

"Now! Now! Now!" I yelled.

But running backward while sliding your finger across your phone's screen doesn't make for accurate throws. We were missing left and right. And up and down. I'm pretty sure I launched one Net to Russia. We retreated all the way back to Grandpa Tepper's backyard.

Meanwhile, Sir FireWing HotPants got angry. Like, burning mad. It opened its mouth and fire poured out like a gasoline stomach flu.

"Whoa!" I yelled as the fire went over my head. I bent backward like I was playing the World's Scariest Limbo Game.

The monster aimed its line of fire at Willa. She gracefully executed a ballet knee drop, rolled, and popped back up once the fire had passed. It turned its head toward Charlie, who'd jumped behind the shed, using it as a shield.

So the fire lit up the shed. Again. That thing wasn't having a good day.

We had to regain control of the battle, but it was hard when we were dodging fire at the same time. I would barely get my phone aimed when the

FireWing's flame breath would come my way again and I'd have to duck and roll and start all over. I'd never get an accurate shot off!

"I've got this!" someone battle-cried from behind us.

I turned and saw Jason running this way. He was pulling a green hose with him, the one Grandpa Tepper used to water his garden.

"No!" Charlie yelled. "Stay back!"

But Jason kept coming, ignoring his brother's pleas. He charged past us and right up to the monster he couldn't see, only stopping when a line of fire came shooting out at him. He unleashed the power of the hose, and a stream of water doused the flames coming from the FireWing's mouth.

I couldn't decide if it was the bravest or dumbest thing I'd ever seen.

In a fit of rage, the monster roared and lashed out with its talon, picking up Jason from where he stood and raising him into the air.

It turned out it was the dumbest.

Jason let out a horror-movie-worthy scream. The FireWing opened its mouth. Whether it was going to cook Jason first or just swallow him whole, I didn't know. I only knew we had one second to make our move while it was distracted by its tasty treat.

"Ready . . ." I yelled.

The three of us stood in position, phones aimed, hands still.

"Now!"

We launched simultaneously and the three shots were perfect. Our BattleNets landed right on the FireWing—and Jason—but when the monster *zapped* into that wonderful beam of light, Jason was left behind. He dropped through dead air and hit the ground with an "*Oof!*"

Charlie rushed over to his side. "Are you okay?"

Jason sat up slowly, rubbing his shoulder. "That thing was going to barbecue me!"

Willa let out a low whistle. "You're lucky we were able to catch it with simultaneously accurate shots. That was close."

Jason sat, stunned, staring at the three of us. "So that stuff you said at the pool really was true. You've been catching monsters. Real monsters."

"Yeah," Charlie said, his face reddening with embarrassment, pride, or both.

"You guys are, like, heroes." Jason's voice was tinged with something I'd never heard from him before. He'd always talked down to his little brother. But right now he seemed in awe of him.

Jason awkwardly scrambled up to standing. Then, still swaying on his feet a bit, he reached out a shaky hand to Charlie. "I'm sorry."

Charlie's Adam's apple bobbed as he swallowed hard. Then he took his brother's hand and shook it.

"I don't understand," Jason said, his voice tight. "You could have run away when the monster was distracted. But you stayed. You risked your life to save me. After everything I've done to you."

Charlie shrugged. "You're a jerk, but you're still my brother."

13

I gave Grandpa Tepper his jacket back. It was a little stinky from the smoke, but no worse for wear. I had several missed texts from my mom, each one getting increasingly angrier. I should have checked in earlier. I should have told her I was going to Grandpa Tepper's house. But I didn't, and in the curt thirty second phone call I had with her I realized there was no way she was going to let me stay out any longer.

I hung my head. "I have to go home."

"We probably should, too," Charlie said, motioning at Jason who still had a dazed look on his face.

"But the SpiderFang!" Willa said. "It's going to spawn in fifteen minutes and we know where it is!"

Charlie scratched his head. "Night monsters spawn at seven p.m. and disappear at six a.m. How about this? We sneak out early in the morning. Let's meet at five thirty a.m. We capture the SpiderFang. Then we go get pancakes and celebrate Wolcott becoming completely monster free."

"Now *that* sounds like a plan," I said. Even Willa agreed.

As we walked Willa to her house, I couldn't stop thinking about how strange it was to spend time with her after everything we went through. Other than Charlie, she'd been my closest friend. When she dumped me to hang out with "cooler" girls, my heart was broken. And every time she saw me in school and said some mean insult, it broke again. But now here we were working together. It hadn't been as bad as I was expecting. Maybe we could . . .

No, I told myself. *Stay focused. Monsters first. Friendship drama later.*

I stopped by Mrs. Sweeney's house on my way

home to get paid for walking William Shakespaw and immediately used that money to buy more Hypnosis Tonic. We'd need all the help we could get with the SpiderFang. Even with three of us and the Tonic, it might not be enough.

At five thirty a.m., the sun still wasn't up. It was technically morning, but the deserted dead-end road was just as creepy as at midnight. The only building on this street was the new middle school, but it was empty in summer. We were alone out here. No cars. No people. Just us—and a SpiderFang.

"Of course, we have to search for the scariest monster in utter darkness," Willa complained. "Of. Course."

The huge middle school loomed in the distance, a reminder of what I'd have to face if I survived today. Our footsteps echoed off the asphalt. The road was eerily silent. No birds, no crickets, nothing. Maybe the monster ate them all.

A bush to the left of us shook as we neared it. A cat jumped out and tore down the road in the opposite direction, screeching and baring his teeth as he ran. I exhaled and willed my heart to stay in my chest.

"Well, that was unpleasant," Charlie said.

We slowly kept moving, eyes peeled. As we reached the end of the road, we stopped at the historical marker, a plaque built into a slab-like stone. It read:

NEAR THIS SPOT STOOD
THE WOLCOTT HOUSE OF JOHN WOLCOTT,
OUR TOWN'S FOUNDER,
UNTIL THE HOME BURNED IN 1849.

The school was to the right behind a large parking lot, too far away. If the SpiderFang hung out near the marker, he wouldn't be that far. He was probably in the woods. I stared at the darkened tree line. It could be anywhere in there. A tingling feeling went up my spine.

"I read a review of that new restaurant on the moon," Charlie blurted out.

What new restaurant? I thought. *They don't have a restaurant on the moon.* But then I realized he was telling a joke. I held back a groan. "What did the review say?"

"The food was great," Charlie deadpanned. "But it lacked atmosphere."

I gave him a pity chuckle.

"What is *wrong* with him?" Willa grumbled.

"He tells science jokes at inappropriate times," I explained dismissively. "It's his thing."

A strange noise came from the woods—an unusual clicking.

I rubbed at the goose bumps that rose on my arms. "Let's do this."

We crept into the woods as quietly as we could. I smelled something off. A monster smell, but slightly different than the others. It was sharp and metallic. I shivered as a realization came over me. It smelled like blood.

I shined my flashlight all around us, waiting to see two red eyes looking back. But other than the smell, it seemed like we were alone. In our world, spiders knew how to hide. They waited until their prey got snared in their web; then they came out. I wondered if the SpiderFang behaved the same way.

The beam from my flashlight caught something glinting between two trees.

"Guys," I whispered. "There's something there."

We stepped up to it in awe. The spider web was big enough to catch a cow. The intricate design shimmered in the moonlight. I'd have stopped to appreciate its artistic beauty but I was more concerned with its creator.

Snap.

A twig broke behind us. *Please be a person. Please be a deer. At this point, I'd take a bear, actually.*

We turned around slowly and simultaneously gasped. The SpiderFang stood on its eight black, furry legs, staring at us with glowing red eyes and fangs that dripped with goo. It was huge; taller than a person and twice as wide.

"Maybe it's a vegetarian spider?" Charlie suggested hopefully.

The SpiderFang hissed in response.

"Okay," I whispered. "Let's all remain calm."

Willa let out a bloodcurdling shriek.

"Maybe calmer than that," I said.

Willa and I stood frozen to our spots, but Charlie backed up to put distance between himself and the spider as he pulled out his phone. Two steps, then three, then—

"Stop!" I screamed "Watch out for the—"

Spider web.

It was too late. Charlie had backed right into it. He flailed and pulled but that only seemed to get him more stuck.

"Help!" he yelled. "It's too sticky! I can't get out!"

"Start launching," I told Willa. Then I dashed to Charlie's side, careful not to get stuck myself. I grabbed his one free arm and pulled. He wouldn't budge. The web was too strong.

"Need some help here!" Willa yelled.

I looked over my shoulder. Willa was trying her best, but the SpiderFang couldn't be caught by one player throwing basic Nets. She needed me. I looked back at Charlie.

"Go," he said. "Take it down. Then come back and get me."

He was right—it was the best plan. Once the SpiderFang had been dealt with, I'd have all the time in the world to free Charlie from the sticky web.

I came back to Willa's side and starting launching Nets of my own. But the SpiderFang ducked and dodged, easily knocking the Nets aside with any of its eight legs. We needed more people. We needed Charlie.

"We're dead," Willa said, her voice shaking. "We're dead!"

She was starting to panic. I had to find a way to keep her calm. "We're fine," I assured her. "I have a plan. I'm going to launch the Hypnosis Tonic, and that will give us a few moments with its defenses down. Then we'll get it!"

I selected the Tonic from my arsenal and held a shaky finger over it. Then I swiped. It landed right on the SpiderFang's head. Direct shot! A haze came over it.

"Now's the time!" I said.

But Willa didn't answer me. She didn't launch any Nets.

She ran.

"What are you doing?" I yelled, confused.

"Getting out of here alive!" she called back.

I was stunned. Willa had used the brief momentary advantage of the Hypnosis Tonic to get away, not to help fight. And now I was facing the SpiderFang alone. I shook my head, forcing myself to move past Willa's betrayal and not waste any more time. I launched a Net. As soon as I'd completed the throw, I knew it was a perfect shot. This was it. I was going to save us all.

The Hypnosis Tonic wore off while the Net was in midair.

Wonderful timing. Just great. The monster knocked away my perfect throw. Then it hissed loudly, saliva dripping from its long fangs. It was *really* mad now.

The sun had started to peek over the horizon and cast its morning light through the woods. Better for me to see all the horrific details as the SpiderFang advanced toward me. The short black fur ruffled on its legs as it walked. Its mouth made terrifying clicking sounds as its jaw opened and closed, eager to eat my face off.

I tossed throw after throw, but it was useless. I was outmatched. For every step I took backward, away from the spider, it took two toward me. It was closing in.

"Run!" Charlie yelled. "It may not chase you because it has me!"

"I'm not going to leave you!" I cried.

"I'm telling you to! Leave! Run!"

The SpiderFang was almost on me now. My mouth went dry. I launched Net after Net as I stepped backward, only to trip over a tree root.

My body went flying backward, hitting the ground roughly. The SpiderFang hissed and clicked with delight. I was dinner and Charlie could be saved for dessert. It leaned over me, mouth gaping wide, fangs dripping. I winced, bracing myself for pain.

And then it was gone.

I blinked, squinting against the morning sunlight shining between the trees. There was no one else here. No one had come and saved me at the last minute. What had happened? I gazed down at my phone and realized that it was six a.m. The nighttime monsters despawned at six. I'd been saved by the time.

I hopped up to my feet, dusted off my legs, and turned to Charlie. And then my heart sank down to my feet. Because he wasn't there. The web—and Charlie—had disappeared with the spider.

14

veryone has a Big Fear. You know . . . spiders, snakes, and darkness. My mom's was bees. She saw any yellow-and-black winged insect and she ran away screaming, arms flailing. My dad's was seaweed, which sounded strange, but if you'd ever had it suddenly wrap around your ankle you'd understand. But I wasn't scared of any of those things.

My Big Fear was losing Charlie.

I had nightmares sometimes that Charlie and his

family moved away. Every time, I woke up crying. Charlie had been my best friend for so long. We saw each other every day. He'd been by my side in elementary school, and I didn't think I could survive middle school without him. And now I might lose him forever.

How would I explain this to his parents? *Charlie got caught in a giant spider web and the monster from my favorite mobile game came to life and ate him.* Yeah, that would go over well.

At first I hadn't understood why Charlie disappeared. He should've been left behind, like Jason when the FireWing went *POOF*. But after I thought about it, those were two different experiences. The FireWing had been captured. That monster no longer existed in our world; it was back in my phone. But the SpiderFang only despawned. It was still out there, waiting for seven p.m. to spawn again.

So the question was this: Would Charlie respawn with it? Or had it killed Charlie already? Was it eating him right now?

I couldn't stop crying. Thankfully, my dad had left for work early and my mom was busy with non-stop conference calls in her office, because this level of snot and sobbing would not go unnoticed. After losing Charlie this morning, I'd walked home and snuck back up to my room. I'd climbed into bed and wrapped my arms around my knees. I didn't want to talk about it. I couldn't.

But after an hour or two of pity partying, I dried my tears with the back of my hand and got to work. I opened my laptop and started reading about spider behavior. One tidbit stuck out. Some spiders don't eat their prey right away. They wrap it in spider silk and save it for later. I read a lot of other terrifying things about paralyzing spider venom, what that venom does to the inside of the prey, and how exactly a spider "eats" the prey. But I shoved those horror shows out of my mind.

The point was we had a chance. And even a small chance was better than none.

Charlie's parents were working all day, and they'd just assume he was out playing the game with me. I had to go back to the SpiderFang's lair tonight at seven and get Charlie back. But I couldn't do it alone. Jason believed us about the monsters now, but he was no help if he couldn't see them.

I pulled out my phone and sent a text to Willa.

I may be mad at you, but I still need your help!
The SpiderFang will respawn tonight at seven.
Charlie might still be out there. I can't do this
alone. Please.

I waited for a response. When staring at my
phone didn't help, I cleaned up the pile of clothes
on the floor of my room. Then I waited some more.
I Googled spider behavior again to search for anything that could help me and only found fuel for my
nightmares. I texted Willa again. I Googled "positive thinking" and waited more. Still no response.
All day long.

The front door opened and closed as my father
returned from work. A while later, he called up the
stairs that dinner was ready. Tears blurred my vision.
The whole day had passed and I was no closer to a
solution. I had no plan, but I still had to go. I had
to try. Charlie needed me, and I would not turn the
other way. I would be there no matter what.

I stopped by the bathroom to splash cold water on
my face and make myself look a little bit less like a
person who'd been bawling off and on all day. Then
I descended the stairs and strolled into the kitchen.

Be totally normal, Bex. Don't think about your best friend's life hanging in the balance. It's just another night.

Dad swiveled around and waved a spatula at me. "Ready for my famous meatloaf?"

"Sure am!" I said with forced enthusiasm.

Dad wore an apron that said: **WARNING. DAD'S COOKING.** I think it was supposed to be funny, but my dad was actually a pretty good cook so the joke didn't really apply. Mom swooped into the kitchen and dropped a bundle of packages on the counter.

"Sorry I'm late." She slid into the seat across from me. "That call lasted forever."

Dad placed a platter of meatloaf and potatoes in the center of the table. "Were you able to negotiate a new bulk price for those charms you wanted?"

"Yes!" she exclaimed. "And the necklaces I have planned for those are going to be a huge hit with my customers."

We each served ourselves and dug in. I really wasn't hungry, but if I just moved my food around my plate, they'd know something was up. So I forced myself to take a few bites.

"What did you and Charlie do today?" Dad asked.

A lump formed in my throat. "The usual."

As if she sensed something off in my voice with her mother-radar, Mom cocked her head to the side. "Bexley, is something wrong?"

I took a big gulp of milk to procrastinate answering. "No," I said, wiping my mouth with the back of my hand. "I'm just tired."

She thought for a moment, tapping the end of her fork against her plate. "Maybe you should stay in tonight. We can watch a movie, make some popcorn—"

"No!" I cut her off, more loudly than I intended. I softened my voice. "Charlie and I have superimportant plans."

"What are these super-important plans?" Dad asked.

I shrugged. "It has to do with the game."

Dad's mouth tightened. "I really think you need to take a day off from that. You're missing the whole world around you."

"Yes," Mom agreed. "I might have to insist that you stay in tonight and do something different."

Panic rose up my throat. I *had* to be there tonight. *Think, Bex, think.* Whining wouldn't work. Talking back definitely wouldn't work. I remembered that Mom had really liked it when I was responsible. Adult-ish.

I folded my hands on the table. "How about we make a deal?"

Mom and Dad shared a look. "Continue," she said.

"I made a promise to Charlie that I would play the game tonight. I don't like to break promises. But I do understand that I've been playing the game too much. So, how about this? I keep my promise to Charlie and play the game tonight. And then tomorrow, I give the game up. Forever."

Mom's eyebrows rose. "Bexley, I didn't mean that you had to stop playing forever. Just give it a rest sometimes."

"I will, I promise. Tomorrow."

Dad smiled like he was impressed and nudged Mom with his elbow. Then she turned back to me. "Okay. We have a deal."

I let out a sigh of relief. "Thanks."

Mom squinted her eyes like she was examining me. "Did you forget sunscreen today? Your face is kind of pink."

That was from all the crying, actually. "No, I wore it."

"You should put more on before you and Charlie go back out."

I giggled in spite of myself. "Mom, the sun's setting soon. What am I going to get, a moon burn?"

Dad burst out laughing, sending a piece of half-eaten potato flying across the table. Then we were all laughing. And for that one moment, it seemed like everything was normal.

Everything was not normal when I left the house a little while later. I was so used to going places with Charlie by my side, it felt weird to walk alone. Not to mention I was heading to the new middle school, a place that I intended to walk with Charlie every day. I couldn't imagine a future without him.

Think positive, I scolded myself.

But a little voice in the back of my head said, *Think logically. You have no chance.*

I hated that voice.

I reached the quiet road. It seemed even more desolate this time without Charlie and Willa. Even the cat from the bushes wasn't around. I passed the middle school parking lot and the historical marker and stared at the edge of the woods. Fifteen minutes until spawning time.

Stepping into the woods, I quickly oriented myself. It was easy to find where the web had been. I could still see the signs of battle on the ground—footprints, scattered leaves. I was surprised there weren't burn marks from Willa's shoes when she tore away so fast.

I slid my backpack off my shoulder and dropped it on the ground. I pulled my phone out. Ten minutes to go. My heart pounded wildly in my chest. My breathing came a little too fast.

Willa's betrayal during battle was one thing, but I couldn't believe she never even answered my text. The only people I knew who played the game had already refused to help us or couldn't help us. I sank to the ground between two trees, feeling more lonely and hopeless than I ever had before.

I let out a pitiful sigh.

"That doesn't sound like a person who's about to save her best friend from a SpiderFang." I stiffened at the sound of Willa's voice and jumped up to my feet. Turning around to face her, I couldn't get ahold of my emotions. I was relieved that she'd supposedly shown up to help—and also angry over the sting of her betrayal.

167

"You ran," I said through gritted teeth. "I needed you. Charlie needed you. And you ran."

"I was going to get eaten!" she exclaimed. "I'm not as good at this game as you are. I had no chance against that monster."

I was momentarily stunned by her admission that I was better than her at *anything*, but I didn't let that cool me down. "So why are you here now?"

"To help."

I rolled my eyes. "You're just going to run away again when the going gets tough."

"Not this time."

I put my hands on my hips. "Oh, yeah? Why not?"

She grinned. "Because this time I brought an army."

15

warily followed Willa. Just outside the edge of the woods, lining the entire end of the road was . . . everyone. I gazed across a sea of familiar faces in the half-light of the setting sun. They all stood, phones readied.

Mrs. Dorsey was in a wheelchair, her broken leg sticking straight out in a bright white cast.

"But you just got out of the hospital!" I said.

"I still couldn't let you do this one alone," she said with a sweet smile. She held up a phone with an NFL case. "I just had to borrow my husband's phone."

Old Man Humphrey leaned against a silver walker with tennis balls at the bottom. He had friends on either side of him, each with their own walkers. I gave him a shocked look.

He shrugged. "You'd be surprised, but *Monsters Unleashed* is the talk of the Senior Center."

I hadn't expected to see any kids from school, but Riya Bedi had come home from science camp and Andy Badger from the Boy Scouts trip. Steve Pak must have come straight from a baseball game in a rush because he still wore his uniform. Isaac came home, too, and seemed to have brought a couple friends with him. They all had their phones out, ready for battle.

And then there was Marcus Moore.

He stood there all tall and cute, and I had to remind myself what a jerk he'd been on the phone. He looked up at me with a shy grin. I'd never seen him act shy about anything.

"Sorry I didn't believe you," he said.

I crossed my arms over my chest. "But you believed Willa?"

"No, I didn't believe her either. One of my friends called me, screaming his head off about seeing a real monster downtown. And he doesn't even know you guys. So I realized it wasn't a prank. Sorry I didn't get here sooner."

Marcus looked at me with those hazel eyes and long eyelashes, and my heart revved up. "Fine. You're forgiven," I said.

"The fact that you were willing to come here today all alone and face off against a SpiderFang . . ." He whistled. "Bex Grayson, you could be the bravest person I know."

I smiled so wide it nearly took up my whole face.

"Hey, Bex!"

I turned. It was Jason and the pack of wildebeests he called friends. He put his fist out for me to bump.

"I only half understand this," he said. "But *I'm* the only one allowed to pick on my little brother."

"Yeah!" his friends echoed, arms in the air.

"But you won't be able to battle the monster," I pointed out. "You can't see them unless you've played the game a bunch."

"That's why I stayed up all night playing it," he said. "After the FireWing experience, I wanted to be able to help out."

"You did?" My eyes widened. It was sad that the nicest thing he'd ever done for his brother was play a mobile game. But it was progress.

One of Jason's friends stepped forward. "And I've been playing the game all summer but never wanted to admit it."

"Me, too," said the other friend.

Jason shook his head in mock disappointment, smiling at the same time. "Guess we're all nerds today."

My throat tightened as tears threatened to spring to my eyes. Everyone was here to help me save Charlie. It was amazing.

By the time I got back to Willa, I was an even bigger ball of feelings.

My eyes glistened. "You did this?"

Willa chewed on her lip, presumably to stop herself from smiling. "Don't get all emotional on me."

"But why didn't you text me back?"

"I was busy calling people, visiting people, twisting arms."

Gazing over the crowd, I shook my head in disbelief. "I can't believe you got them all to believe you. And to show up!"

She grinned. "I can be very persuasive."

That, I knew. But this time it had actually worked in my favor.

"I'm sorry," she said, so softly I barely heard it.

As I looked into the eyes of my ex-friend, I knew she wasn't just talking about bailing on us yesterday. She was apologizing for all of it.

"Why did you do it?" I asked.

"I already told you. The SpiderFang was going to—"

"I'm not talking about that."

Willa let out a long breath and looked down at the ground. "I was sick of being unpopular. Ignored. Invisible."

I rolled my eyes. "And the cool girls liked that you were pretty and an awesome dancer and that made you feel good. I get it. But you could have been friends with them *and* friends with me. You didn't have to kill our friendship and be mean to me."

"But I did," she said. "We're starting middle school. I wanted a blank slate. If I was going to change, really change, I had to leave behind my old life. Completely. I had to push you away."

"Well, you did a great job at that." I glanced at my phone's clock. It was almost battle time.

Willa reached out for my arm. "T-Bex . . ."

I shook my head. We'd have to continue this another day. It was time to save Charlie.

"Okay, people," I said, raising my voice high enough to be heard. "I'm going into the woods to get Charlie from the web as soon as it spawns. You stay in formation and launch, launch, launch. We'll be counting on you."

And I could only hope that Charlie was still alive.

I returned to the spot where the web had been and unzipped my backpack. I pulled out my mom's gardening shears. Any moment now, the clock would switch over to seven. Any second . . .

With a buzz and a quick flash of light, the woods lit up. I put up a hand to shade my eyes but after only a second or two it was dark again. I brought my hand down slowly, almost scared to look.

The glistening web was back, strung between the same two trees. And inside of it, was Charlie.

"You're alive!" I whisper-screamed.

Charlie turned his head left and right, as much movement as the sticky web would allow. He was breathing heavily and his eyes looked like they were about to pop out of their sockets. "What's going on? Where's the SpiderFang?"

"I don't know. But it can't be far. I'll have to do this quickly."

I lifted the heavy shears and started cutting. The first string of the web resisted and needed a few tries with more force, but I eventually got it to snap.

"Get out of here," Charlie hissed. "I can't let it kill you, too."

"We're fine," I said, working on another string. This stuff was pretty strong considering it came from a spider's butt.

"I've done the calculations, Bex. Alone, we have exactly zero chance of survival. Zero, Bex!"

"Then it's a good thing we're not alone."

I snipped the last string that was holding Charlie to the web and he fell to the ground with a thud.

Meanwhile, behind us I heard Willa lead the crowd in a battle cry. "There it is! Get it!"

The crowd roared, and I heard the electronic sound effects of over a dozen gamers playing at once.

Charlie looked at me like I'd grown an extra head. "What's happening?"

I grinned. "Come see."

We peeked around a wide tree trunk, and what we saw made my heart swell inside my chest. The

SpiderFang was at the edge of the woods by the marker, dodging and ducking throws from an army of gamers. They all fought together. Boys and girls. Young and old. Friends and enemies. All working together to save one boy. I'd heard my parents use the word *community* a lot but didn't really get what it meant until now.

I'd thought I was all alone, but I wasn't. So many people had risen to the occasion when it really mattered. I thought I was getting my best friend back, but I was really gaining so much more.

Willa stood in the center, directing them like an orchestra. "Mrs. Dorsey, the Hypnosis Tonic, now!"

She launched it, and a haze fell over the spider. This time no one ran.

"Just like we planned!" Willa yelled. "Ready? Three . . . two . . ."

"Want to get in on this?" I asked Charlie.

He nodded. "Definitely."

We stood up, pulling our phones out like dueling outlaws in a western movie. And by the time Willa had yelled "one" we were part of the team. We launched our Nets from behind the SpiderFang. It was surrounded.

And this time, it was overcome.

With a zap and a flash, the SpiderFang lit up and disappeared. I felt my phone buzz as the monster returned to its rightful place. The crowded cheered.

Charlie and I ran over and gave them all high fives. Then I gave Charlie the biggest hug ever. Jason lifted him off his feet in a squeeze that nearly crushed his lungs. Even Willa got in on some hug action. Though she said, "Eww, gross" after and wiped her hands on the nearest tree to get the nerd cooties off. But that didn't bother me. Nothing could bother me.

I had my best friend back.

16

settled the charm bracelet into tissue paper and gently wrapped it. The tissue paper went into a cute little bag with my mom's company logo on it. Then the bag went into the waiting package. I sealed the package up and placed the correct mailing label on top.

One down, ten million to go.

Mom returned to the dining room with an armful of more orders and plopped them on the table. "How are things going, Miss Assistant?"

Now that I'd given up the *Monsters Unleashed* game, I had more time for other things. Namely, making some side cash. Mom paid me to be her assistant, and I kind of loved it. I found the work relaxing after the experience I'd been through. And I was saving the money for whatever new game I ended up wanting to buy.

"It's going well." I put a hand on a pile of packages. "These are ready for the post office. I'll have more ready later today."

Mom pulled out a chair and sat beside me. "I really appreciate all your help this week."

"No problem." I checked out the next order. Another charm bracelet. That was definitely the top seller. I slid a piece of tissue paper off the stack and started pulling the order together

"You haven't been playing games much lately," Mom said.

"I'm spending a bit more time in the real world."

Mom smiled at that.

I was done with the *Monsters Unleashed* game but not done gaming. I was just on a short break. Willa had dance. Charlie had his science experiments. Jason had pushing people and catching balls. We all had our thing. Gaming was mine. My brain whirred with ideas for apps and games I wanted to create myself someday.

After college, I could even move back to Wolcott because Veratrum Games was headquartered here. And while this game had gone a little haywire, I couldn't wait to see what Veratrum came up with next.

The door opened and closed, and Charlie came waltzing into the dining room, his eyes scanning the counter for stray food. "Hey, Bex. Hey, Mrs. Grayson."

"Good afternoon, Charlie!" Mom said.

"Hey, Charlie." I slapped the mailing label on the package and placed it in the done pile.

He gazed at the mess on the table. "Are you going to work all day?"

"No, she's not." Mom looked at me. "I appreciate all of your help, but it's Saturday. Go be a kid. Have fun."

Well, if Mom was forcing me. I jumped up from my seat and walked with Charlie to the front door. "What do you want to do?"

"Want to head to the park?"

Nerves fluttered in my belly. I really hoped he didn't want to play *Monsters Unleashed* again. I thought he knew I was done with that game. "To do what?"

He shrugged. "I was thinking we could go on the swings."

I laughed. "The swings?" I hadn't sat on a swing in so long. But the idea sounded kind of relaxing. Just what I needed after the week we'd had. "Sounds great, actually."

We walked to the park just like always, and I tried not to think about how close I'd come to losing my best friend. I'd asked him afterward what it was like to wait twelve hours to be respawned. He'd said that it was like no time had passed at all. One second he was in the web watching helplessly as the SpiderFang leaned over me, ready to go in for the kill. Then the next second, I was standing beside him with a pair of gardening shears.

It made me feel better that he hadn't been tortured those twelve hours while waiting for me to save him. And considering the experience he went through, Charlie was just as happy as ever.

We reached the park and grabbed two swings next to each other. I pumped my legs and soared through the air higher and higher until I was laughing and

Charlie was, too. There wasn't a cloud in the sky and the gross humidity had broken. It was a perfect summer day.

"Did you hear about the book on antigravity?" Charlie asked with a grin. "People can't put it down."

I laughed so hard that I made an embarrassing snort sound. I was so glad to have Charlie—and his stupid jokes—back.

"Bex!" someone called. "Charlie!"

I put my feet down and slowed the swing as Marcus Moore ran toward us. His phone was in his hand. My stomach flipped over like a pancake. We got all the monsters! There were none left! What could be wrong now?

But as he got closer, I saw that he was smiling. He looked quite excited, actually.

He stopped when he reached the swings and took a second to catch his breath. "Did you guys try the new game Veratrum just released? It's so cool!"

My heart pumped a little harder with excitement. A new game? From the makers of *Monsters Unleashed*? It was probably amazing.

But then I looked at Charlie, grinning in his

swing, tilting his face up to catch rays of sunshine. There would be plenty of time for the new game.

"No, we haven't played it yet," I said. "Maybe tomorrow."

"You're missing out!" Marcus yelled as he dashed away, phone in hand.

Charlie and I sat in silence for a while in the way that only best friends could. I watched kids running around the park, parents chatting over their coffees, families enjoying the beautiful day. We'd saved the town, and most of its people would never even know they had been in danger. It made me feel kind of awesome.

"Are you still worried about middle school?" Charlie asked.

"Nah," I said, truthfully.

After saving the town from snarling, toothy monsters, how scary could it be?

183

Acknowledgments

A writer never creates a book alone. For helping me make this one, I'd like to thank:

My agent, Kate Testerman, who is amazing. I'm so lucky to have her on my team.

My editor, Christina Pulles, and the rest of my Sterling Squad—Hannah Reich, Ryan Thomann, Ardi Alspach, Hanna Otero, Terence Campo, Sari Lampert Murray, and the entire sales team. Thank you for your hard work and enthusiasm. The Gamer Squad would not exist without you, and for that I will be forever grateful.

Joann and Lauren Chandler, for the ballet terms, dance jokes, and overall awesomeness.

All the writers, readers, booksellers, librarians, teachers, and members of the KidLit community whose love of books keeps us all going.

My parents, for being my biggest cheerleaders. I personally apologize to anyone who has been stalked by them in a bookstore and has had one of my books shoved into their hands.

Ryan, for not minding that he ended up with a crazy mom who makes too many jokes, sings too loudly in the car, and dances in the living room. Out of all the kids in this great big world, I'm so glad I got you.

Mike, for listening to all my crazy ideas and being my first reader. You're my love and my best friend, and I'm so happy to share our lives together.

And the rest of my family, the outlaws, and friends—too many to name—for being a part of my life. I treasure every one of you!

Ready for more gaming adventures?

Here's a sneak peek at

GAMER SQUAD 2

Close Encounters of the Nerd Kind

1

was going to be late for school if I didn't leave soon, but I couldn't move from my spot. The alien invasion had begun. I watched through my phone's screen as UFOs drifted down from the blue morning sky onto my front yard below.

I banged my finger against the screen, firing lasers at every enemy spaceship until they were all gone, and the words **YOU SAVED THE EARTH** flashed on the screen. Smiling broadly, I looked up to high-five my best friend, Charlie Tepper, but he wasn't there.

"Hey, Bex, did you win?" he called from his front yard next door.

At some point, he'd stopped playing and had wandered over to toss a football with his older brother, Jason. That was a sight I'd never get used to. Until recently, Jason's only contact with his brother was to bully and insult him. But after we nearly lost Charlie in an, um, monster incident, Jason had been nicer. And it helped that, once he actually began spending quality time with Charlie, Jason realized that his nerdy little brother had a secret. Surprisingly, Charlie had quite an arm on him. So Jason had made it his life's mission to teach Charlie everything he could about football. I didn't think Charlie would be interested for longer than a day. But it had lasted the rest of the summer, and he'd even joined the middle school football team. Though I still clung to the hope that the whole thing would be a passing fad.

"Of course I won," I said as I strolled over to them.

It wasn't as conceited as it sounded. I'd be the first to admit the things I was bad at (which were many). But gaming wasn't one of them. I was an awesome gamer, and I'd even started to teach myself how to code using online apps. It came easy to me, like science did to Charlie. Though he spent less time doing chemistry experiments in his basement these days.

"Heads up!" Jason yelled.

I ducked just in time to avoid getting a football lodged in my nostril.

"We should go," Charlie said. "See you later, Jason."

Jason was a freshman and thankfully the high school was in the opposite direction. I liked walking to middle school with Charlie alone. Lately it seemed like the only time we got to really talk. We only shared one class together—science. And lunch was so crowded that sometimes in all of the chaos, we didn't end up at the same table.

Things had been so much simpler in elementary school.

"So what did you think of that science homework?" I asked, hefting my backpack higher on my shoulder.

"It was pretty easy." Charlie kicked at a pebble and it flew a few feet in front of us. "The field trip tomorrow night sounds awesome."

"Yeah, it does." I kicked the pebble farther. This was a game we played most mornings. We'd find a pebble and take turns kicking it all the way to school.

He took a turn, launching the pebble ten feet down the sidewalk. "You're really into *Alien Invasion*, huh? Do you think it's as good as *Monsters Unleashed?*"

The makers of *Alien Invasion*, Veratrum Games, had previously created a game called *Monsters Unleashed*. We'd been totally obsessed with it over the summer. Until some of the video game monsters got *really* unleashed and we had to save the town from real live snarling beasts.

"It's not quite as good, but it feels safer." I laughed, and he joined in.

Both of us had vowed never to play *Monsters Unleashed* again. But I was happy when *Alien Invasion* came out. It was another augmented reality game, which meant that when you were playing, it looked like the game was taking place in the real world. It used the phone's camera and graphics card to do the trick. And there was nothing like battling video game aliens in your school parking lot.

Even our science teacher, Mr. Durr, liked the game. If you played at night, there was a really cool extra feature that "was actually educational," he said. When you held the phone up to the sky, a star map filled in, showing exactly what stars and planets you were looking at. I'd learned a lot about astronomy while I protected our planet from fake aliens.

"You still haven't played at night yet," I pointed out.

Charlie's parents had finally agreed to get him a cell phone after he'd joined the football team, so that he could text them when it was time to pick him up from practice. When we used to play mobile games together, he always had to borrow his mother's phone. It was great that he now had his own—if he ever had free time to use it.

"I've heard the game's ten times cooler at night," Charlie said.

My face lit up as I thought of an idea. "How about tonight? Eight p.m. My backyard. The weather app this morning said it was going to be clear skies. Perfect for playing!"

Charlie held the school's front door open for me. "I can't. I have football practice after school. And then I'm going out for ice cream with the team. And then I'll have to do all my homework."

My heart sank into my gray Converse sneakers. I followed him into the school, feeling like I was losing my best friend. We'd been inseparable since I'd moved in next door when we were five. We didn't even mind when other kids teased us about being boy/girl best friends. But since we started middle school three weeks ago, things felt like they were changing. Or, more specifically, Charlie was changing.

"Hey, do you have any new science jokes?" I asked. "You haven't told me one in a while."

Charlie raised his eyebrows. "You hate my science jokes."

"I don't *hate* them."

He gave me a look.

"Okay, I used to think they were a little annoying," I admitted. "But, strangely, I miss them."

His science jokes were totally dorky, and he sometimes came out with them at inappropriate times. But everything was suddenly moving too fast. I just wanted one thing to stay the same.

"Well, I can't think of any right now," he said with a shrug.

Then the bell rang so loudly it made my ears ache.

"Gotta go!" Charlie called.

Kids darted left and right, squealing with their friends. I shuffled toward my classroom, head down, feeling like a lost puppy. Then I felt a shove, like someone had pushed my backpack. I looked around, but the hall was chaos. It was probably an accident, some kid bumping me while trying to squeeze by.

I settled into my seat in English class and put my backpack on the floor. But then I noticed something. A white piece of paper had been shoved into the side pocket. I glanced around. No one was paying any attention to me, as usual. So I slipped the note out and unfolded it. When I saw what it said, my heart did a cartwheel.

YOU'RE INVITED
TO JOIN TGS. TONIGHT,
THE COMMON, 7 P.M.

What was this? A secret group? I had no idea. But I couldn't wait to find out.

2

School passed in a blur, and I sped through my homework all afternoon. I couldn't wait until seven. I was so excited to find out what TGS was. It was definitely taking my mind off the way things were with Charlie.

I slid into my seat at the dinner table as my father put out a platter of chicken and potatoes. My dad was an incredible cook. Even plain old chicken and potatoes tasted awesome. And he loved coming home from the office and slipping on his apron. He said cooking helped him "decompress." I didn't really understand, but his process ended with tasty noms, so that's all the mattered.

Mom settled onto the seat beside me, typing wildly on her phone.

"A phone at the table?" my dad said with a wink. "Really?"

Mom chuckled but continued typing. "One second. I just have to finish this last email."

The "no phones at the table" rule had been created for me, so that I'd stop gaming long enough to put food in my mouth. But now that the personalized jewelry business Mom had started out of her home office had taken off, she broke the rule more than anyone.

"Okay, I'm done!" she announced and pushed the phone away.

I stabbed a roasted potato with my fork and blew on it until it cooled. "How was work?"

Mom let out a breath that made her bangs flutter. "Busy."

"My day was nonstop meetings," Dad said with a sigh. "But I'm home and decompressed!"

See? He really liked that word. I held up a finger as I chewed through a bite. "Pretty good. I'm excited about the field trip to the observatory tomorrow night."

"That sounds wonderful," Dad said. "Is Charlie excited, too? I know he's always been into the sciences."

At the mention of Charlie, I felt my shoulders sag a bit. My parents knew that he'd joined the football team, and I was sure they'd noticed we were spending less time together. But I tried not to show how much it was bothering me.

"Yeah," I said, my voice cracking. "I think he's excited."

My parents shared a look.

"We've been thinking," Mom said carefully. "Maybe you need to . . . widen your circle of friends."

I could tell by the way they tiptoed around the conversation that this was something they'd discussed ahead of time. Something they were worried about. I hated it when my parents worried about me. I mean, I knew it was their job and all, but I was fine. Everything was fine.

I cleared my throat. "That's a good idea. Actually, I'm meeting some kids from school at the common tonight after dinner."

"Great!" Mom said.

"Wonderful!" Dad echoed.

The rest of the dinner conversation spiraled into current events and politics, like it sometimes did. But I was glad the spotlight was off me. Having to talk to my parents about my social life was always so awkward.

I helped my mom with the dishes and grabbed a light jacket. September in Massachusetts was unpredictable. It could feel like summer one day and midwinter the next. I didn't know what to expect when I went to the common. And I wasn't just talking about the weather.

The walk was quick and uneventful, though strange. I hardly ever walked downtown without Charlie. Wolcott Common was an open, grassy area where kids played and people had picnics and stuff. There were always at least a handful of people milling about. So I was surprised when I got there and found . . . no one.

I glanced at my phone. It was seven o'clock. I wasn't late. Was the note a trick of some kind? Did the TGS people change their mind, whoever they were?

"*Psst . . .*"

The sound came from the pretty white gazebo. I squinted and could make out someone's shadow.

As I walked toward it, my nerves prickled. Maybe it wasn't such a great idea to go meet a stranger, even in a public place.

But when I got closer, I realized the sound wasn't coming from a stranger after all. And then I got even more nervous.

Marcus Moore stood in the center of the gazebo, hands in the pockets of his jeans, looking super cool in his black Veratrum Games T-shirt. I'd had a crush on Marcus since, well, since I knew how to have crushes. He was one grade ahead of me, wicked smart, and the best gamer I knew. Of course, along with those skills came an unfortunately large ego. And the fact that he didn't care what anyone thought of him was both adorable and horrible because he could be annoyingly sarcastic at times.

"Is this . . . the TGS meeting?" I asked.

"No. It's a sewing circle."

Like now. This was one of those times.

I rolled my eyes. "If you're going to be a jerk, I'll just leave."

He quickly descended the steps of the gazebo to the grass. "Come on. I was just joking. You're so serious, Bexley Grayson."

"It's Bex. You know that." He probably also knew that I hated my full name. And that was probably why he used it. But I wouldn't crack a smile or give him any sort of reaction. I stood, stone-faced.

"You're probably wondering what that note was all about," he said.

"Nah. I came here to look at the stars."

The side of his mouth lifted up. "Looks like two can play that game."

Dang it. I couldn't complain about him being sarcastically rude if my reaction was to do it right back. "So," I said, evening out my voice. "What does *TGS* stand for?"

"The Gamer Squad," he answered. "It's an invitation-only, elite group of the top gamers in town. And after how you handled the *Monsters Unleashed* debacle, we think you're the perfect fit."

My eyes widened. Was this heaven? Had I died and gone to a perfect place?

"Th-that sounds incredible," I stammered. "What do you do?"

"Well, we're relatively new. But we game together, obviously. We try out betas. Play around with some coding so we can build our own apps."

I had to stop myself from clapping with excitement. "That sounds awesome. We're in. We're totally in!"

Marcus raised an eyebrow. "We?"

"Charlie and I." I almost added a *duh* because it should have been obvious.

Marcus's expression turned serious. "The invitation was only for you."

All of that excitement drained out of me like a dead battery. I couldn't join a gamer group without Charlie. We were gaming partners. Even now, when he was busy with his new hobby, I couldn't imagine heading off to secret gamer meetings without him. Would I have to lie about where I was going? If the group found an awesome new game, would I have to play it without him? All summer I'd been worried that middle school would tear our friendship apart. Whether that happened or not, it certainly wasn't going to be my doing.

"I'm out, then," I said sadly.

Marcus's mouth dropped open. "You're rejecting me? I mean, us?"

I shrugged. "I can't join without Charlie. He's my best friend."

Marcus snapped his jaw shut and his eyes flared.

"Have fun playing games by yourself, then. Because your supposed best friend has already moved on."

He stormed off in a huff. I couldn't believe he'd gotten so upset. I wasn't rejecting him personally; I just couldn't join his group if they weren't also inviting Charlie. It wasn't the right thing to do. Marcus should understand that. He knew what Charlie and I had been through last summer with the monsters.

As I turned to watch him march away, I saw what he'd meant when he said Charlie "had moved on." A bunch of kids, including my best friend, ambled down the sidewalk past the common in their football gear. Practice had ended and they were walking to the Ice Cream Shack. It wasn't a surprise, really. Charlie had told me about it. That was why he couldn't play *Alien Invasion* with me tonight.

It hadn't bothered me too much at the time. But watching him now with his new buddies, laughing and shoving one another while I stood in the darkened common alone . . .

I couldn't help but wonder if Marcus was right.

Look for all three

books at your favorite bookstore!